POTTERVILLE MIDDLE SCHOOL

Loggerhead

eas-y books

FROM E. A. SEEMANN PUBLISHING, INC.
Miami, Florida

Loggerhead by Jack Stark
The Sponge Pirates and Other Stories by Jack Stark
Adventures on the Airboat Trail by Ida Haskins

JACK STARK

Loggerhead

E. A. SEEMANN PUBLISHING, INC.
Miami, Florida

All places and persons in this book are fictitious.

For my grandchildren—

Virginia Lee, Kimberly Ann, and Chuck

Loggerhead

1

Ponce sat at the end of a rickety Key West dock pondering his future. His loggerhead sea turtle had died in the Turtle Pens and he would have to catch a new one.

The fifteen-year-old Cuban boy stood erect and hitched his worn and frayed hemp rope belt a bit higher on his slender body while he glanced with a frown toward the sleeping town. At his brown, shoeless feet a wooden bucket held a coil of rope. This he would use to lasso a wild sea turtle offshore.

Ponce's ears caught the familiar sounds of sea gulls crying shrilly in their morning flight and barnacles clacking as the tide rose on the dry boards of the dock. The dock squeaked and groaned as the water expanded its loose planks. Across the harbor the Tortugas and Grand Cayman fishing fleets had not yet shown life.

The Turtle Pens where he earned his living wrestling giant sea turtles lay to his right on the shoreline almost out of sight. His loggerhead had died in the pens days ago and the men had dumped it into the harbor waters.

Footsteps on the dock jarred Ponce from his thoughts. He turned and spied Miguel Jimenez racing across the silver-gray boards. Ponce sat and dangled both legs over the nineteen-foot skiff below him in the water. Miguel came up and settled down beside him. He was puffing from running hard. His black eyes shone like tar pits. They reflected orange lights from the sun when·he turned to face Ponce.

"I thought I was late!"

"You're the first," Ponce replied.

"Where are the others—Marco and Jorge?"

"Not asleep, I hope," said Ponce. He knew very well how he would need them all if he was to catch a sea turtle large enough to wrestle. He knew where to find a loggerhead on the offshore reef. He had seen it there several times lately as it watched the beach. Evidently its mate had gone ashore at night to lay its eggs in the sand. Possibly it had been disturbed and left. It would return again and again until the eggs were laid.

Ponce wore maroon colored shorts held up by the bit of hemp knotted about his middle. Like the Greek sponge divers in Tarpon Springs, he did not use aqualungs to dive, just a face mask. He was proud that, like them, he could stay submerged for minutes without air.

Miguel was fourteen, a year younger than Ponce. He had dressed in a white, loosely fitted nylon shirt that Ponce knew would get extremely hot in the sun. He had on khaki slacks and tennis shoes.

Ponce spoke: "How is 'Satisfaction'?" This was Miguel's name for his goat.

"She is home. I tied her up inside the yard."

Ponce recalled that a goat was not too unusual in Key West where the Cubans owned fighting cocks, ducks, dogs,

12

cats, caged birds, turtles, guinea hens, white rats, and fat 'possums. These assorted pets often outshrieked their owners, who lived mostly on their front porches. A female goat was just a part of the colorful scene in the island city at the end of the Florida Keys.

Ponce smiled as he thought of Miguel leading the goat around on a rope every day delivering milk to his many customers. This *was* unusual. At each stop, using a variety of small glass jars and cooking pans, he milked the goat, "Satisfaction." It was very convenient, if not sanitary. But no customer yet had complained of the milk not being fresh. Today "Satisfaction" remained at home and tied. A day off.

The summer air grew warmer and the white shrimp boats reflected sunlit patterns from ship to ship. The skiff below Ponce slapped to the rising water and strained against its line. He patiently awaited Marco and Jorge who soon appeared, bearing disturbing news. Ponce listened as Jorge, a part-time Tourist Train guide at only thirteen, excitedly told him about the Oceanic Aquarium crisis that same morning.

"The pasty-faced, red-headed kid who works sometimes at the aquarium for Mr. Foster is in trouble," Jorge said between gulps of air.

"He told us to find you," Marco added. He had on his red Key West Athletics baseball hat with the long visor shading his sharp face. Marco was the youngest of the turtle hunters. He was only twelve.

"It's the tanks again," said Jorge. "The fish are dying in the tanks."

Ponce's heart stood momentarily still. When it began beating again, he asked what he dreaded. "Why?"

"No one knows," they both chorused. Marco tugged at his duck bill cap.

13

"Your father is there now helping where he can," added Jorge. "He is even less help than old Mr. Foster." He laughed. Not bitterly. Just a young boy's laugh remembering something very funny to him.

Ponce realized things must be desperate if the red-headed boy had sent for him. The red-head tried to understand about the saltwater fishes and the exhibit tanks, but always seemed to be doing things wrong at the Oceanic Aquarium. Ponce's father's greatest wish was that his son would work there instead of wrestling the large and dangerous sea turtles in the Turtle Pens. Ponce considered any aquarium work dull. Thus, the red-headed boy had been hired by Mr. Foster as a last resort.

Marco blurted: "Mr. Foster is going crazy trying to save the fishes still alive. He can't discover the trouble. I think it is lack of oxygen." He shook his head from side to side.

"I must go," said Ponce with finality.

"The sea turtle?" Miguel's eyebrows shot up.

"It will wait." Ponce turned toward shore.

Old Placido, opening his fish shop, "The Red Snapper," gazed in awe as three lively boys, with Ponce leading them, raced along the tiny sidewalk. They almost knocked him down as he stepped out his door into the new day. Then they were gone in a cloud of dust.

He shook his head. Each generation, he thought to himself, seemed to be different from the one before it. He remembered his father mentioning it to him many times. He took off his glasses, blew on them, wiped them clear with a rag, and polished the fine gold rims. Then he gave a deep sigh and yelled fiercely at a cat trying to slip into his half-open door. The yellow and white alley cat fled, its tail straight in the air. Placido glared evilly at it, then thought about Ponce. What was that boy turtle wrestler up to now, he asked himself. Nothing moves that fast in the Key West summertime. Morning, noon, or night!

Placido sighed. The boy did not have a mother to guide him. He had known Ponce's mother, who died when Ponce was a baby. Now the boy only had his father. It was a constant struggle for both of them, he knew. Ponce was headstrong.

"Turtles," he said aloud. He slammed the screen door shut to keep out the cat. The Red Snapper was open for business.

Ponce and his group flew down the street toward the big white building that housed the Oceanic Aquarium. Its two black windows, located above the wide and dark open door, looked like the two eyes and the gaping mouth of a manta ray. It was toward this monstrosity they ran. When they entered the dim interior they saw a sight they would long remember.

Along the damp concrete walls were brightly lighted tanks filled with strange fishes. Many of the colorful blue, yellow, red, black, multi-striped, and dotted fishes floated belly up on top of the tanks. As the boys' eyes became accustomed to the darkness, they noticed several people rushing around trying to help.

One was Mr. Foster in his white tennis shoes and his disheveled white hair, who moved helplessly about the tanks. The other was Ponce's father. He paced silently like a black stork.

The pasty-faced kid leaned against the wall as if in shock.

2

It was plain to Ponce what had happened. The aquarium's fish tanks were not bubbling. Somehow the air had been cut off. Why? How? These questions leaped into his mind. He turned to the red-haired boy and seized his shoulders.

"How did this happen? "

The boy appeared stunned. Seeing Ponce arrive, however, had made him recover somewhat. "I was adjusting the valves," he said. "I might have turned the wrong one."

It was evident, to Ponce, that he had.

"Ponce! " Señor Alvarez finally caught sight of his son, and he was relieved that the boy had arrived to aid them in their trouble. Mr. Foster could use Ponce's agility and know-how now. He wiped his brow.

"I will see what I can do," replied Ponce quietly. He turned away so that his father would not see the rush of mist to his eyes. He felt so badly about the dying fishes. They were unbelievably colorful and alive. He ruled out sabotage. No one could kill them on purpose. It had to be an accident.

"Am I glad to see you!" shouted Mr. Foster, rushing up to Ponce. The boy noticed that his clothes were soaked and grimy from grease. He evidently had been climbing around in the pipes and beams overhead. The air pipes led in from the outside at the rear of the aquarium. They were located high overhead in the rafters.

Ponce knew that Mr. Foster had not solved the problem. The old man looked worn and tired, and his rimless spectacles hung crookedly from his bony nose. He resembled a fish hawk in a tree which had just had a silver mullet slip from his talons and wondered where it went.

Without any more delay Ponce asked for a pipe wrench. When it was handed to him he climbed up into the dark maze by a stepladder. It was dirty work, and the footing was tricky along the open rafters and pipes.

He searched for a pipe marked with a red painted band. This would be the main air conduit that led in from an air compressor banging away loudly outside the old building. This pipe could be forced shut by turning its main valve clockwise. If the boy hadn't done it, then Mr. Foster might have an unknown enemy. He glanced down at the small group below him. The pasty-faced youth had not joined them.

I wonder what it would be like to work for Mr. Foster all the time? He needs an experienced person. Then these things would not happen. I must not think such thoughts. I must fix this valve and get back to my boat. The turtle is more important to me.

Then he found the main pipe. He saw the valve. It was locked tightly, just as he had thought. His hands could not turn the round metal handle that let in air. It looked as though it had been purposely locked shut. It *could* mean Mr. Foster had someone who did not want him to stay in

17

business. The boy was very clumsy, but he was not skilled enough to force the main valve shut. Or was he?

Ponce took firm hold of the wrench and clamped the jaws around the metal handle. Holding on with both hands, he leaned back and turned. The handle moved slightly. Then again. It seemed frozen. He put his full strength into it. It broke off at the shank. Ponce almost fell from the pipes as the cast metal gave way.

"Watch out," he yelled to those below. The small group on the main floor scattered. The broken valve handle clattered to the concrete floor.

"What is the matter, Ponce?" his father called up, alarmed.

"I broke the valve. It was forced shut. It won't turn at all now." The now useless wrench dangled from his hand.

He saw Mr. Foster stare at his beautiful tanks. Some of the fishes sought oxygen near the top of the water, swimming in slow circles. They worked their mouths. The valve had to be fixed, Ponce knew. It was up to him or all the fish would die. The red-haired boy had disappeared.

"Jorge," yelled down Ponce. His friend looked up into the dim interior. He could barely make out Ponce's face. "Jorge, run down to the corner gas station and ask the man there to loan you a hacksaw. Also a foot or two of garden hose. But hurry. There isn't much time left." Jorge fled the aquarium, his sandals flapping noisily.

"Miguel." It was Ponce again from atop his perch. Miguel moved across the aquarium where he had been studying the tanks.

"What is it?" He wanted to help if he could.

"Miguel—go out back and shut off the air compressor. You can stop the motor with the large, rusty screwdriver hanging on the wall. The main switch to the motor was broken long ago and never fixed. Put the screwdriver against the sparkplug and also the motor's exhaust pipe. This will kill the engine." Ponce hesitated. "Remember, you must touch metal to metal." He glanced down worriedly. "But hurry," he added.

Miguel raced out back onto the dock. The strong morning sun struck his face and blinded him for an instant. He knew the metal shed that housed the air compressor and ran toward it. He located the old screwdriver where Ponce had said it would be. He took it in his hands and placed the tip on the sparkplug. He touched the metal shaft to the exhaust pipe. He was careful to touch only the wood handle with his bare hands. The compressor could give a mighty shock.

The noisy motor sputtered, coughed several times, and died in a puff of blue smoke. He had shut it off. Miguel realized that all air had now been stopped. He wondered if Ponce was doing the right thing. He shrugged. Ponce was capable. He must have a plan.

When he reentered the aquarium he noticed that Jorge had returned with a hacksaw and a two-foot section of garden hose. He was handing these up to Ponce from the tall ladder. Miguel turned again to the fish tanks and began to count. A large grouper was gulping surface air.

Overhead Ponce worked furiously. He took the hacksaw in his two hands and cut off the end of the pipe leading into the still jammed, broken valve. His hands flying, he moved quickly to the pipe section ahead of the valve. He cut in furious strokes. Shortly the entire valve and its short ends of pipe fell to the floor below. It had been completely cut out.

Working against time, Ponce took the garden hose and

cut a short piece with the saw. It was slightly longer than the open break between the cut out section of pipe. He fastened the hose to each end of the pipe. It fitted nicely. He jammed it hard. When he was satisfied he yelled down to Miguel to restart the motor. Miguel raced out the back door. He recognized the start button. It was red. He pushed it, and the familiar cough of the engine roared across the harbor.

Instantly the thin hose in front of Ponce leaped into action. He watched closely as the air surged through on the way to other pipes and eventually to each individual tank. He tested it at each end. It had to hold. If it blew off—! He would prefer not to think about it, he told himself.

The hose gripped the rough-cut sawed edges of the pipe and held. The throb of life-giving air surging through the hastily made hose connector felt good to Ponce's hands gripping it. The air rushed into the fish tanks, bubbling up out of small pipes in their bottoms. The air bubbles rose quickly with their supply of fresh oxygen. Fishes stirred into motion and began to swim feebly. The crisis was over.

Ponce climbed down wearily from his high perch. His legs ached from his forced position straddling the pipes. He was weary from his struggle with the valve and the sawing. A wave of renewed strength passed through him when he realized he had saved the tropical reef fishes. It was an achievement to be proud of. Later, someday when he had the time, he would fix the pipe correctly and put in a new air valve for Mr. Foster.

"It will stay," he told his father. A grin came over his face as he noticed his father dressed for work at the Chamber of Commerce in his black silk suit with a once-white panama hat now yellow with age. He looked out of place among the fish tanks. His pointed black shoes gleamed. He smiled at the boy studying him.

20

Mr. Foster walked up to ask Ponce what had gone wrong. Ponce waited before he spoke. Much of what he saw looked as though it was no accident. The pipe and valve had been purposely forced shut after being tightly closed.

"It was no mistake," he advised the old and watery-eyed aquarium owner.

"If I ever get my hands on him . . ."

"You probably won't," Ponce said.

Ponce scuffed a bare foot on the damp concrete floor. He turned to leave. Then he added: "You have an enemy. Something else could happen. Even worse!"

3

Red-haired Cliff Waggle, who owned the Turtle Pens and Cannery, walked out to the saltwater docks where he could see the lazy flat sea.

His mind was occupied with twin problems this morning. One was that the boy Ponce had lost his loggerhead turtle. This meant the boy could not wrestle in the pens until he had captured another large one. It was a serious loss to them both. It would hurt business. Many people came to the pens just to see the young Cuban wrestle the giant sea turtle.

Another concern was the return of the turtle schooner *Andy Hanks*, supposedly boring up on its back leg from Costa Rica and Grand Cayman with a full load of big green sea turtles. Waggle needed this supply badly for making turtle soup. Last week a New York hotel had placed a large order for the soup and he hadn't been able to fill it. His pens had remained empty for weeks except for the loggerhead, which had then died. The *Andy Hanks* had been gone for more than a month gathering its catch from natives on Caribbean beaches.

Cliff Waggle had come to Key West from a small Connecticut village eight years ago. He had owned a tiny gasoline station which did well in the small town. But he tired of snow and long gray winters. He had sold the station and headed South.

He bought the Turtle Pens and the rusting soup cannery building and went to work. In time he turned the pens into a sensational tourist attraction in downtown Key West. He had added a ticket booth and charged admission for tourists to see the turtles.

The turtles were herded much like cattle in the enclosures that had access to the sea through stout posts which allowed salt water between them. The pens were very deep, but many of the giant sea turtles swam on top in view. Their sharp, breathing snorts when they emerged could be heard a half block away.

Waggle had put up signs along the highway—SEE THE TURTLE PENS—and later added BOY WRESTLES KILLER TURTLES. He recalled this stroke of genius, smiling down at the calm bay this summer day. The tourists thronged in to see Ponce fight his loggerhead daily in the largest pen. It was an exciting thing to observe. The boy had lithe speed and strong hands. The giant turtle had superior weight, strength in its flippers, and a fierce beak that could take an arm off in a single snap.

"Why not?" Waggle inquired of his friend, Dr. Barbour, one day on the street shortly after adding Ponce's act. "The tourists admire the boy's skill and the turtle's fight. The extra money helps me to keep open. Mad money, you might call it." Waggle grinned comfortably.

"Mad—right!" exploded the old Key West physician. "I worry about the boy getting hurt, or, worse, drowned. Those turtles are vicious." He glanced quizzically at the red-haired businessman. Waggle kept silent.

23

Dr. Barbour pursued his plea. "Come see the boy get hurt like in a bull fight. Put that on your sign!" He took his eye glasses off his nose, folded them, and placed them carefully in his top pocket. "You could also add some new modern methods to that cannery operation. I do not like to think about the crude ways used in turtle butchering. It is too barbaric. The heavy axes and the sharp knives. AAAAH!" He spat disgustedly in the gutter.

Waggle enjoyed this kind of banter. His New England soul rose to the occasion in a battle of wits like this. His words, sharp and to the point, came out in a nasal twang: "Yew don't like all the killin' and the blood. Yew do eat meat, I recollect."

The doctor agreed quickly, defensively. "I do. But today's modern methods of butchering meat have no resemblance to what you are doing in that cannery. I object mostly to your hanging onto old-fashioned methods."

"I have no funds for scientific frills," Waggle whined. "I make a bare living."

"Does the killing ever worry you?"

"No."

"I shall not eat turtle steak any more."

"You had better give up the turtle soup too."

"I shall, sir."

"Good day, doctor."

"Good day, Waggle."

The old doctor stumped off down the street feeling as though he had finished second in a horse race. Which he had. As usual.

As Waggle stood alone on the dock this morning gazing out to sea staring for the sight of the *Andy Hanks*, he remembered his talk with Dr. Barbour. It had often crossed his mind. Maybe, someday Ponce and the turtles would become such an attraction he could close down the cannery. He would consider it. He knew he would have to if the *Andy Hanks* ever stopped sailing. It was his only source of the green turtles for soup.

Sally Barlow, attractive, middle-aged, and supporting two small boys by working in the gift shop, approached Cliff Waggle on the dock. The wind picked up suddenly and flapped Waggle's pants legs. She saw him scratch one leg with the other. He was irritated over something serious, she said to herself. His irritation always made him break out in hives. He was a hard man and given to impatience with those around him. The combination was not easy to handle.

"Shall we open the ticket window now?" she asked softly. The leg scratching continued in silence. Up and down, up and down. The hives were active today. Must be the overdue schooner, she thought. And Ponce.

"Might's well," he replied. The fact he did not snap her head off was good news to the staff watching from inside the gift shop. Each day they tested his moods. Today was Sally's turn.

"It's eight o'clock, yew know," Waggle snorted. "Time to get some money in. It won't drag itself in the door or bust down any windows." He looked sidewise at her through his light blue eyes set beneath shaggy brows. The brows were as tough and wiry as he seemed to be. He noticed Sally looked drawn this morning. Must be the night heat. It had been difficult for her to work after her husband had been killed by a falling tackle block on a shrimper. But Sally was a good and loyal worker, even Waggle admitted.

"I hope it cools off some today," he continued.

25

"It will. I feel it now—a fresh breeze."

"The *Andy Hanks* is late."

"It will come in today. I feel it in my bones."

"The tourists don't come out when it's so hot. They stick close to the air-conditioned motels and swimming pools." Waggle felt a slight puff of wind on his scaly neck. It cooled the perspiration lying there in the creases.

"It will be a fine day," Sally offered optimistically. "And Ponce might get a new turtle." She noticed him start.

"And I might fly to the moon in a rocket," Waggle snorted.

He paused, and then continued. "Open up and we will see how good a forecaster of weather you are. The U.S. weather bureau only knows 'hot and rain.' They change it every other day to bat fifty percent. It's *either* one." Waggle smiled. His mood was somewhat better. Sally had cheered him up.

"Yew quit yore jokin' " she said in jest, mocking him. Then she quit the scene in a flurry and walked toward the cool gift shop. As she entered she nodded her head up and down. That meant everything was all right with "THE MAN." The help fled to their tasks. She opened the front door and put a young girl with long, stringy blonde hair inside the ticket booth.

"Hippie!" she said. "Hope she don't steal Waggle blind." She muttered to herself as she worked. Help was hard to get these days.

Cliff Waggle kept a few monkeys in cages, a tame gray squirrel, an otter from the Everglades, and some captive alligators in a sunlit courtyard. There was also a square-shaped, concrete-sided open pool where he put some young immature sea turtles for the tourists to handle and photograph. In the entrance he had chained a raccoon with its left ear missing.

"Your place is a might mixed up," a tourist lady in a flopping straw hat had told him one day on leaving.

"I like it that way," he retorted. She huffed out.

Waggle tried to give the tourists what they liked. He was a man without an artistic soul trying to make it in a hard world that gave him too many problems. He was plain and blunt-spoken. He ran his place by simple standards.

The gift shop stood open at the front on the dusty street. Shutters that lifted up and latched overhead revealed a formica-topped counter. The shop held all sorts of curios and shells and some lighted fish tanks in which small reef fishes were displayed. Pieces of staghorn coral from the reef, bleached a brilliant white, were displayed for sale. Blowfish hung from the ceiling with their bellies extended like balloons. Yellow lightbulbs reflected from inside.

It might all change someday, Waggle thought. It *might* make a good operation without all the killing. He studied his empty pens. The water was all he saw.

"Where is that danged-blasted schooner?"

4

The giant loggerhead lay a mile offshore Key West in a thick raft of sargasso weed. Its shell resembled a small island in the brown mass of seaweed where terns walked about picking at tiny crabs and shrimp with their flashing orange beaks. The white terns flew with jerky motions and made thin piping cries over the old turtle. Their heads turned down toward the water as they flew, unlike sea gulls, which flew with their heads straight ahead.

The sea giant had swum fourteen hundred miles from below Puerto Rico in the Caribbean. The Gulf Stream had aided it some by its steady surge northward from the equator. The loggerhead was in no hurry. It had passed by the hot, sandy tip of Yucatán following the big blue Florida current into the Gulf of Mexico. At the Dry Tortugas it had rested several days. The ancient red brick fortress laid a steady light at night across the water. Lobster boats, mostly run by Cuban fishermen, came close but avoided Fort Jefferson's protected waters. Nearby Loggerhead Key's blinking lighthouse flashed all night. Then an inner urge took hold. The sea turtle headed directly for Key West seventy sea miles away.

At Key West the old turtle found what it had been looking for and settled down. Its mate had gone ashore again last night to lay one hundred moist, white eggs in the sand. In sixty days they would hatch in an eruption of mass motion from beneath the sand as the small turtles fought together toward daylight. The old turtle had been as small once.

When the newly-hatched turtles emerged from the sand like silver dollars with flippers, they would all head together toward the sea. They were vulnerable to most creatures, especially sea gulls, wild dogs, raccoons, opossums, pigs, and man. They would head directly for the water in a squirming traffic jam, and when they finally felt wet sand their flippers would jerk by instinct. They would swim forth boldly and dive beneath the waves. In the water they had to avoid being eaten by a number of fishes, including the bold crevalle jacks and pompano.

Those that survived would grow up in the sea. Only females ever came ashore again and then only to lay their round eggs in shallow nests scooped out of the sand by their hind flippers. After they laid the white, rubbery eggs they covered the nest with sand and debris and left. The young were on their own to grow up.

For a year the young turtles would seemingly disappear in the sea. Then, in a year or two, they would start appearing at the same nesting grounds where they were born. Here, in time, they would mate and fight for the attention of the females. Their migrations across hundreds of miles of open ocean still is a mystery to man. Some say they navigate by the stars since they can locate a tiny island without fail.

The old loggerhead bore sharp barnacles on its back. It thrust forth a yellow head and breathed. The turtle had no fears any more. Only very large sharks would attack it. Or a man. Not since it had been small and helpless had it felt fear. But at night the sea giant slept with its flippers folded along its shell to protect them.

The day was hot and the sea around lay like glass. The turtle waited for its mate to return. Then they would swim away. Its mate had been disturbed and prevented from laying its eggs twice. The male's lids now slid closed. It slept atop the water in the weed bed. It had recently eaten a meal of fish. It opened its mouth wide, then closed it.

5

Ponce's turtle-catching skiff was nineteen feet long and specially built. It had high flat sides and two mid-center seats for rowing. Across the stern lay a large metal roller on pins that was used for hauling in nets by mullet fishermen. The bow had a special seat which had a cabinet built beneath it to hold ropes and anchor. The seat lifted up as a top for the cabinet.

The wide boat had a cross-planked bottom. It was not easily tipped, thought Ponce, who stood in the stern observing his crew: Marco up front, Miguel and Jorge rowing. They both bent their slim bodies to the long oars.

The sea lay flat as molten steel. The early morning puffs of wind had already left them. Ponce heard the bow suck in the tide as they moved. It made a gurgling sound he liked. It meant he was at sea again where he belonged. The sound brought it home to him.

They were already past the green waters of the channel and taking a shortcut over some shallow bonefish flats. As they rowed toward the brownish-toned flats the turtle schooner *Andy Hanks* passed them in the main channel. Ponce could see it was loaded with green turtles, the kind that make the best turtle steak and soup. It had loaded the last of them at Grand Cayman where extensive turtle sea farming was going on. Ponce watched it approach the Turtle Pens where it would unload several hundred turtles.

Ponce wanted a loggerhead—not a green turtle. Loggerheads were meat eaters and fierce. The smaller green turtles ate turtle grass which grew in pastures on the bottom. They were more gentle. Green turtles were not such fighters in the pens as the loggerhead.

Now and then the skiff passed over some sand holes gouged out by the current. These were light green since the sand reflected the sunlight more than the brownish grass that covered the flats. In the sand holes they could see brightly colored fishes darting to and from the banks. Now and then an owlish grouper looked up at them in the boat.

Miguel stopped to remove his white nylon shirt which had heated his body. The boat turned in the tide and almost threw Ponce off balance. "Row, Miguel," snapped the boy turtle wrestler. "You will have me in the water yet!"

Miguel laughed and took up the heavy oar again. He and Jorge soon had the boat on a straight course. The water wasn't deep, only about six feet. It would not have been a serious mistake except at sea. Ponce knew at sea you avoided mistakes because they had a way of piling up into tragedy. Many a boat had been sunk by a lighted match near gas fumes or a wrong turn into an oncoming breaking wave.

"Is this where you get your sponges?" Marco asked.

"No," replied Ponce. "Out farther in fifteen feet of water where it is clearer, and the ocean washes them gently."

32

"I have never seen the reef." Marco added. "That is where you often dive?"

"Yes," replied Ponce. "I dive for sponges, coral, and shells for the Turtle Pens. They sell them in the curio shop."

Marco gave his friend an admiring glance. He reached up and tugged the long visor of his red baseball cap with KWA in white letters on the front, standing for the the Key West Athletics. Like all Cuban-Americans he loved baseball with a passion. Ponce looked so self-reliant standing against the blue sky, Marco thought.

Ponce carried doubts with him today. First, his crew was raw and unused to the sea. Then there was the serious matter with his father. His father had spoken again yesterday about Ponce's turtle wrestling. He did not like his son to hunt for them in the open ocean. Ponce could not understand this because of his speed in the water and his mastery over the huge beasts. Once he leaped in and grabbed the shell near the neck he knew who would win.

"There is not too much danger in it," he told his father.

Señor Artistado Alvarez worked as a counter clerk in the Key West Chamber of Commerce Building in Mallory Square. The single story brick building fit into the new restoration scheme of the small city that Union troops occupied during the Civil War. Many old buildings had been restored and the white painted conch houses were protected. Any newcomer had to guarantee to keep them in perfect shape and not change their unique style.

Ponce's father pushed his case: "I don't mind you diving for shells and sponges," he said. "I am afraid of the big turtles, even in the pens. But at sea—alive! " He shuddered.

Ponce thought of this as the boat sped out to the open sea. He noticed flecks of brown sargasso weed floating and knew larger rafts of it would be found. It was a good turtle

33

sign. The boat stopped. Jorge now changed places with Marco. Jorge sat in the bow. A tall windblown cloud grew anvil-shaped ahead of them. Ponce made a mental note to watch it. It could produce strong winds and rough seas.

He called out to Jorge.

"How come you got the day off from the Tourist Train?" The boat rocked with laughter. All of them knew Jorge worked part time on the rubber-tired train that ran through the Key West streets full of sightseers.

"The owner gave me the day off. With pay," added Jorge who still had on his lettered cap, TOURIST TRAIN GUIDE.

"How come?" Ponce persisted. He was forgetting about the aquarium where his father wanted him to work.

"I earned it." Again, laughter rocked the boat.

"How?"

"I saved a dog."

"A dog?"

"Yes. A very small one owned by a rich woman. It had no hair on its body and it wore a jeweled collar."

There was a murmur from the boat as the four boys pondered the ways of the tourists who had more money than any of them had ever known.

Jorge did not explain what had happened. Yesterday he had leaped out of the train and caught the small dog which had dashed off the curb into its path. It wasn't until he had returned it to the owner that he felt the grip in his stomach. The woman who owned the small Mexican hairless had bought out an entire trip on the train for herself and her friends at Waterfront House. She was very rich.

"You give this boy a day off," she said to the owner.

"I shall, madam," he replied. He was a busy man.

34

"With pay."

"Yes, madam." He shrugged.

Jorge sat quietly in the bow remembering and holding on now to both sides of the boat with his hands. The boat lifted and fell as they entered the ocean. Long swells had gripped them. He felt somewhat uneasy in his stomach. Like yesterday. He had risked his own life for a dog.

Then Jorge remembered the dog as it licked his hand. The dog had never sensed any danger. It was tiny and lively in his arms. Jorge loved all creatures. He wondered if he could actually help Ponce much when it came to capturing a big turtle. He hated force against any animal.

Worse yet, he wondered deep down inside whether— when the test came and he was needed in an emergency— he would fail his friend, Ponce. This disturbed him as they swept out into the sea.

No one could fail Ponce—ever—he told himself.

The boat rose and fell with the swells. Jorge stole a glance at his tall friend. He would not add any trouble when the capture came.

Ponce needed this turtle. Badly.

6

"I seen your boy going out the harbor in his skiff," said Captain Olaf Anderson of the *Andy Hanks*. He looked down over the rail at Cliff Waggle standing by the wooden turtle pens with their round, rotting posts.

"He's gone turtlin'," said Waggle.

"Must be daft. I got three hundred on board here," the grizzled sea captain replied. Waggle shook his head.

"He only wants a loggerhead to wrestle," the Turtle Pens' owner said. Then he explained to the schooner captain how the boy's turtle had died. The men on the two-master began making fast to the dock. Lines flew through the air. A donkey engine coughed into life.

"Three hundred turtles I got and he goes out in his dinghy to find a special one," snorted Captain Anderson. He had a rough, black beard, streaked with gray, which he stroked as he talked. His nose was strong and prominent and peeled from too much sun. He wore a dirty captain's hat with a black visor.

A gangplank leaned onto the dock and the lanky captain

descended it. His shirt was blue denim and his pants were white duck. He wore black rubber boots which were practical at sea. He tucked his pants into the tops of the boots. Waggle thought it gave him a piratical look.

They both headed for the coolness of the main office where they could enjoy a cold drink.

Behind them they left the confusion of the schooner and its unloading of the three hundred green turtles into the pens. The men sweated in the hot sun as they raised each turtle high into the air by a hook looped into a rope through their front flippers. Lowered to the dock, the rope was cut, the hook was freed, and the turtles were slid into the pens via a wooden chute, landing with a loud splash.

The boat made its monthly run through the tiny towns and Indian villages of Central America where the natives hunted turtles along the beaches. The natives sought them out in small boats and speared their shells or netted them. They tied logs to their forelegs and turned them loose along the beaches. They caught many in a day this way and later returned to claim them since they could not swim very far with the logs hindering them. Then they were put into crude beach corrals made of sticks and wire.

The schooner eventually came along the shore and loaded the turtles onto its decks and inside its hold. Waggle had gone along once. He never forgot the sights and sounds of it. It had been off a black beach in Nicaragua.

At dawn the schooner had stumbled onto a large group of the green turtles swimming together far at sea. The ship followed them. Now and then a turtle would dive, but mostly they continued as a pack. They posted a man on the bowsprit and followed the turtles all that day.

"They are like chickens," Captain Anderson had explained to Waggle. "They leave at dawn for the sea and return each night. I go along with them now to find the nest. Then you will see something."

"How will you ever catch them?" asked Waggle.

"Too deep here," Anderson replied. "We will wait 'till they nest. That is the secret of taking them all."

That night the turtles entered a shallow bay with a nearby beach. Captain Anderson's "nest" was discovered. The sea monsters had led them to the nesting grounds.

Waggle slept the night through thoroughly tired. Sweaty sailors slept in bunks below decks while he and Captain Anderson shared a cabin on deck. By daybreak Waggle was up and watched the men set their long nets.

The men put off from the schooner in their small, round-bottom dories. They had a huge pile of nets strung across the stern of each craft. They rowed away from the schooner and began to lower the nets into the water in a long line across the inlet. They tied each net with a floating cork to hold it up and lashed them all together. The line of nets must have been a half mile long.

Soon the turtles swam out to sea. They were clumsy, lumbering beasts. They blundered unknowingly into the strong nets, where the men yelled and beat the water with boat oars. Soon the noise and confusion attracted sharks. They tore at the nets and the trapped turtles. Blood and chunks of torn flesh floated before Waggle's eyes. Waggle became sick and left the railing. Captain Anderson watched him go with a smile. They each remembered it yet.

"It seemed a colorful picture until the sharks came," he confided to Captain Anderson in his office as the *Andy Hanks* unloaded its fresh shipment. "I hated the sharks."

Captain Anderson nodded his head. He pursed his lips and rubbed his bony nose.

"About the boy, Ponce," he said softly. "You gonna always hold him in bondage?" He jerked his bushy eyebrows aloft.

"Your boat don't look like it has many more trips in it, Captain," replied Waggle. "I might need him and his loggerhead more than you think. I'm building up a good business around the boy. The gift shop gets bigger. The tourists come to see—not to eat."

"The cannery?"

"It, too, is as bad off as your boat."

"That is truly bad!" Captain Anderson sipped his drink slowly.

The two men looked at each other silently. Then they began to laugh out loud.

7

They had come a long way from the distant shoreline when Ponce ordered the rowing stopped. Marco and Miguel rested on their oars. They wiped their forearms across sweaty faces.

"It is very hot and humid on the water," Miguel remarked.

"Yes, it always is," replied Ponce, wiping his own wet forehead.

Ponce reached forward from where he stood and, bending to the center seat, opened a panel on top. He produced a round tub from inside, similar to the one that held the coil of rope. The bottom of this tub was made of thick glass. Ponce handed it to Miguel and told him to place it in the water and look through it.

Miguel did as Ponce suggested. He held the tub over the side with his hands on both sides. His wiry black head disappeared inside, and suddenly a green and lovely underwater world opened before his astonished eyes.

This was Ponce's amazing ocean garden on the outer

reef. It was Miguel's first sight of it. The reef held beauty even he had never dreamed existed. He whistled with amazement. His high-pitched whistle echoed oddly from the hollow bucket.

It was the same as looking through air. The glass inside the bucket was below the surface reflection and glare. It revealed a scene of waving sea fans in the undersea current. On the coral reef below live sponges thrived in various shades of brown, pink, and yellow. The coral itself was brown, as though covered with algae. Now and then a piece of white staghorn coral antlers reached up like the rack on a deer's head. It was a beautiful sight to Miguel.

He noticed small tropical fishes swimming in graceful patterns below near the coral head. Their colors rivaled the brilliant colors in the reef. They collected around the coral head, which resembled a small hilly peak in the green sea, and swam into and out of round holes and crevices. The coral head was sharp and a danger to ships that came too near. It could cut through a steel hull.

One of the fishes Miguel watched was a yellow and black striped sergeant major which darted into and out of the coral head. Fat red groupers with dark spots looked up from the bottom crannies with owlish stares. Jacks patrolled the middle areas, and French grunts with blue and yellow striped faces swam in a solid pack. Gray snappers worked in schools over the bottom, looking upward.

Miguel watched as a large crawfish emerged from a cranny and crossed the white sand. Its long feelers swept the ocean currents, sensing danger. Startled by the swaying head of a green, snakelike moray eel that stuck halfway out of a den, the crawfish moved swiftly backward away from harm. It used its fleshy tail to shoot backward. Otherwise it crawled forward on spidery legs.

41

Miguel studied the sponges growing on the reef. They looked like round balls of bursting cotton and had hollow centers. Tiny minnows often took refuge inside them to escape larger fish that would eat them. It was a strange world he looked at.

Miguel looked up at Ponce standing over him trying to see into the bucket around his head. "It is a miracle," he said.

"Let Marco see," Ponce replied. "Then Jorge."

Miguel quickly removed his head from the bucket. One at a time the boys took turns holding the glass bottom bucket and seeing the wonderful and strange sights of the reef. Its peaceful appearance could fool you, Ponce knew. Any moment it could change with the appearance of a large barracuda, or a hungry shark. At night he did not like it at all and never came out. Even to fish. It was a strange place at night with a strong surging tide and a darkness that depressed him. It was at night, too, that most of the fishes fed.

Ponce also kept the aquarium supplied with sponges to sell to the tourists. He had to haul up the heavy, wet sponges and then bring them in to shore to beat them with a board and dry them in the hot sun. He did this in his backyard, washing them out with fresh water from the hose. His father did not like the smell, but he smiled at Ponce at work over them. Eventually, he knew, they would lose their strong odor.

Ponce usually worked with a sharp sheathed knife in his rope belt. He did not wear an aqualung, only a face mask so he could see clearly. He dived alone on the reef using a woven reed basket. Into this he placed his conch shells and the heavy sponges. When it was full he would swim with it to the top and gulp in air. Ponce could stay underwater a long time. His lungs had enlarged with all his diving, and each time he found he could stay below more easily.

He used a heavy rock to carry him quickly to the bottom. It was tied to the boat with a long rope. When he went over the side he would grasp it in both hands and plummet to the bottom fifteen feet below. He also placed a smaller ballast stone in the wicker basket, which he sent down ahead. When it was full of sponges he removed the stone. He kept more in the boat to resupply it. He made several trips to the bottom this way. Each time he unloaded his catch into the boat he would haul up his diving rock by the rope and take another quick trip below after gasping air.

In far off Hawaii divers used the same trick. In a way Ponce was like these divers. He was fearless in the water and very agile. He was also like the turtles he often hunted. He always had to rise for fresh air, and he swam like a fish. He grinned at the amusing thought.

All the boys were busy with the water glass so they did not at first see the shark. But Ponce did. He saw it and warned them. He pointed at the rough brown fin cutting circles in the calm sea only fifty feet away. They could see the whole body of the shark, especially the blunt head. Yellow eyes glared evilly. It came forward swiftly.

"Wow," said Marco, alarm in his voice. Miguel stiffened and watched the shark's even progress from the depths to their boat. Jorge tugged at his cap. None of them had ever been so close to a shark other than seeing them while fishing from the wharf in downtown Key West. This was different.

"He will soon leave us," Ponce assured them. "It is only a large nurse shark. When he sees what we are, he will go. He is curious—that's all."

Ponce was right. Suddenly the shark gave a thrash of its forked tail and left in a big boil of water. They all breathed easier when he departed. Ponce was glad it wasn't a hammerhead. The hammerhead was a bad shark and might attack. So would a mako. All sharks had bad vision, but good noses.

"Are there any barracudas?" asked Jorge, switching the subject away from sharks.

"There are," Ponce said. "But you never quite see them. But drop a wounded, or hooked, fish in the water. Poof! They are there like a log. Watching you and finally grabbing the fish."

A white tern, with its orange beak pointed toward the water and its black legs tucked into its belly, flew over the boat. Ponce observed it. It was a sign. Sometimes birds led him to a turtle. They sought the bits of fish a turtle left on top the water when feeding. The tern left.

Ponce watched the little bird fly away. Then he spoke: "Do you remember Jimmy Pepper?"

"I knew him," Miguel said. "He lives in Miami now."

"Jimmy's right arm was taken off by a barracuda while he swam in the harbor from an anchored boat," Ponce explained. "He dove into the water almost on top of the 'cuda. It was frightened. Then it turned and struck. Like that!" He slashed one hand across his arm.

Marco did not care for this sort of talk. The shark had been enough to think about. He glanced across the water toward land that suddenly seemed awfully far away. The water beneath the boat looked twice as deep. Streaks of golden sunlight pierced it to the very bottom like rays of the sun piercing trees in a morning mist. Its depths confused him. Marco hoped they would find a small turtle and go home. The land looked safer.

The boat now moved slowly among huge weed beds as Miguel took up the oars and rowed quietly. Marco joined him. They had trouble keeping the drifting weed off their oars. Its stringy arms with air bubbles kept clinging to anything that was near. When the weed slid off into the water he could see small crabs and shrimp dart from it to another clump. It was their hiding place from feeding fishes and birds.

There was life and death every minute on the outer reef.

Ponce now raised a tall slender pole from the floor of the skiff. It had a rope noose at one end that led into the coiled rope inside the bucket he had brought along. His friends watched him anxiously.

"We begin to hunt our turtle," Ponce stated.

"How?" Miguel asked.

"By working around these weed beds across the ocean top. Here a turtle often rests looking like the weed itself. He sleeps safely in his weed bed. It protects him. But we will sneak up and slide this rope over his head."

The air became charged with excitement. Each tired boy came alert. Marco felt the hair rising on the back of his neck. It felt like tiny needles pricking him.

Ponce smiled and gripped the long pole in his tough young hands.

8

Each of the boys in the boat soon discovered turtle hunting was hard work.

They rowed in turn at the oars and Ponce tried to keep them interested. But it was hard work for everyone. Ponce searched the sea and sky for a sign. Most sailors look to the sky for cloud formations and birds to tell them things. Ponce instinctively looked around him for some sign that would bring them success.

Each of them also found out you could row all day and never see a sea turtle. Sharks, rays, needlefish, flying fish and mullet they saw. But no loggerhead stuck his head above the weed on the calm ocean. At times, luck seemed with them. Then just as quickly it vanished. It would be a bobbing coconut or a drifting styrofoam float resembling a turtle head. As the morning wore on Ponce worried more and more about his friends.

It is too calm today. Or maybe the sun is too hot. It is the way of all fishing. I am unsure. None of my friends is used to this problem I am forcing upon them. I may have to give up.

With his eyes now smarting from the salt and sweat, Ponce searched the weed eagerly for a turtle. By noon he too was ready to go back. There were few signs today. The weed bed was empty. The tern had flown off into the blue, blue sky. Even the thunderhead rain cloud had disappeared.

Miguel and Jorge were rowing. Their arms ached from the exertion. It was unlike anything they had done on shore. The silent sea offered nothing but its blazing surface to them. They admired Ponce's courage and stamina. But the sea was winning. The battle was uneven—four boys in a boat against the immensity of the ocean.

"My luck is no good," Ponce finally said.

Miguel nodded in agreement. He wiped his hot brow. The sweat ran down into his eyes. Miguel hoped they would stop rowing and head back to shore. But, since he felt sorry for Ponce and his loss of the big sea turtle, he would wait for Ponce to quit the hunt. He would row as long as his friend wanted.

"My arms ache," said Marco.

"My other end's sore," replied Jorge.

"Miguel?" asked Ponce. "How about you?"

"I shall row until sunset," Miguel stated. "But it seems so useless today." He hung on the oar.

Ponce looked over his tired crew. Then he made a decision.

"We will go home in twenty minutes if we have not sighted a sea turtle," he said. "Give me that much time." They all breathed a sigh of relief.

"Hooray," cried Marco from the bow. Ponce looked at him. Then Ponce smiled. He knew what a relief it must be to have called a time limit on the hunt. Everyone seemed cheered by his decision.

Ponce turned his face to the empty sea. There must be a

big turtle out there. He stood erect in the boat's stern by the roller. His brown body and black hair shone brightly in the strong sun.

Then he stiffened.

He glanced ahead of the bow in the calm water and noticed several sea gulls alight on a weed patch. There were several more there too. The weed had a slight bulge to it. Or did it? He rubbed his eyes. They were strained from the hot glare off the water. Then he saw the huge shell of a sleeping turtle. He noticed the color and size. The large head rested on the weed. He saw the flash of some yellow scales. It was a loggerhead—and it was alone. He was in luck. Usually there were a pair. One usually would watch while the other slept. This old one was alone.

"Quiet," he cautioned his young crew with a low word. The boys looked up at him at first in alarm. Then they noticed where he was staring. Up ahead Ponce had seen something they hadn't. Then they all saw it. A huge sea turtle, its flippers back against its body, eyes closed. They stared in disbelief at the sight.

Ponce moved quickly toward the bow of the skiff over their legs and bodies as they turned to let him go by. He whispered to Marco. Marco also moved ahead to the bow with Ponce. Miguel and Jorge remained in the center of the boat. The skiff crept slowly ahead without any sound. Only momentum moved it ahead to the still-sleeping giant turtle.

Carefully, Ponce took the long turtle-catching pole in his hands. He inched ahead in the boat as it closed the distance between him and the turtle. His brown hands clamped down tightly on the pole until the white showed beneath his knuckles. The noose was hanging loose at the end. The rest of the rope ran back into the bucket behind him. It was neatly coiled.

"Do not speak," Ponce whispered. He held his finger to his lips.

No one in the boat thought of speaking. They all watched as the gap between the small boat and the giant of the sea closed. Then Ponce's arm flicked out and the rope noose slid over the head. The loggerhead had been contacted. It was theirs to fight!

Ponce watched the turtle's head raise high. Then it swung its body and dipped the left flipper deep in the water. It sank sideways, both flippers working now and Ponce yelled out: "We're onto him. Bring in the oars and hang on."

The rope fed through his hands. It burned once, quickly. Then Ponce took a series of quick hitches around the bow stem. He advised his friends to sit low in the boat as he made his way aft. The rope was tied to the stem and the turtle would pull them. The oars came in and the boat moved quickly through the sea. Ponce held onto the rope.

They were on. The loggerhead swam deep in the water ahead as their boat left a foamy track across the water. Ponce wondered now whether he had been wise to tie into such a giant with an inexperienced crew. The turtle was going to give them a ride to remember.

He glanced quickly toward his friends huddled together on the bottom of the skiff. Their excited faces turned to him dispelled any fears he might have had. They were with him all the way.

The turtle tugged and shook the boat. The bow dipped lower in the water with its weight. Ponce climbed out farther on the stern to balance the skiff. He felt the boat shudder with the pull on it. This was a big turtle. His smile grew as he hung on.

He would play it to the end.

9

The sleeping loggerhead felt the rope go tight around the soft flesh of its thick neck.

It had digested its recent meal and was dozing when this new threat came into its life. The sudden rope pull frightened the turtle.

With a snort of defiance through open nostrils, which sent a plume of spray into the air, the turtle surged forward and down, four hundred pounds straining for freedom.

As it raced through the clear water, the depths felt cool against its warm shell. In the first frantic dash to escape from the rope's grip, it managed to pull the heavy boat a few hundred yards ahead. This accomplished nothing except to tighten the rope more securely around its neck.

That choked the swimming loggerhead. It didn't strangle the turtle due to the strong lateral muscles in its throat. The loggerhead slowed and turned broadside to the boat. It was using its weight to break the rope.

The turtle's eyes bulged with the effort. Small fishes

fled wildly, seeing the sea turtle caught and struggling against some unseen enemy. They watched from a safe distance as it fought, dragging behind the telltale rope that led upward to the top of their green world.

Had it been a large shark which had clamped down on its flipper, the loggerhead would have known instantly what to do. It would have whirled in a flash and shut strong jaws down on the vented gill openings through which the shark breathed. The shark would have found water seeping into its lungs. It would have been forced to let the turtle go or drown.

This fight was different. Here was the cunning of man. It was a danger the sea turtle had not before faced.

Trying a new tactic, the loggerhead swam in a full circle twenty feet below the boat's dark shadow. Strong flippers pulled it through the water with the same bull-like tenacity it had shown in the first dive. Now it could see the hated rope curving behind. The loggerhead moved to a much greater depth.

Increasing water pressure on the soft skin between the upper and lower shells felt heavy. The more the turtle dived, the greater the weight became. This was caused by the increasing density of the water at depths. The increasing pressure also helped to choke the sea turtle.

The smaller reef fishes had now vanished. They were hiding in rocky crevices as the drama built. The positions of the vacated fishes were taken over by several large barracudas that hung as menacing wolves in a circle around the stricken turtle. These toothy pirates were waiting to see what would happen to the loggerhead. They moved silently into range from the purple depths. Just as Ponce had said before, they seemed to come from nowhere.

The loggerhead grew weary of the constant tug of the

rope. On one of its turns the barracudas pressed too closely. For a second the rope dangled. The turtle took the nylon between its strong jaws and shut down on it. Savagely.

This new strain on the tough rope was punishing. But it held. Failing in its efforts to break it, the loggerhead tried a new trick. It moved up to seize the rope in a new spot. It bit hard on the rope again. In this odd manner the turtle worked itself nearer to the surface. It tired more and its lungs ached for air.

The loggerhead's big head came out on the surface and its red nostrils swung open quickly to suck in air. Goggle eyes bulged from their sockets. It noticed the boat a few yards away across the slick water. Four brown figures were standing up pointing at him. The sea turtle saw them pick up two long sticks and move ahead. He dived again, dragging the rope.

These struggles for freedom were not entirely in vain. The rope began to fray in several spots where the sharp beak had cut it. But still it held. Once again the loggerhead surged ahead in a straight line only a few feet below the transparent surface so that it could lift its head out to breathe more often. The boat was a heavy burden.

In this manner the giant sea turtle continued to tow the skiff. Now and then the head shot up for air. Then it moved ahead. Trailing along were the curious barracudas that waited and still watched the turtle's struggles. The loggerhead paid them scant attention.

One of the barracudas, more foolish than the rest, made a test lunge at the slow-moving loggerhead's right front flipper below its body. The turtle felt the swirl. It lowered its ponderous head beneath the surface and searched. When it saw the 'cuda it whirled inward in a flash of rage.

Free of the pull of the rope, for an instant, the logger-head struck out and bit down on the fish's thick body. There was no escape.

The strong beak cut clean through the startled 'cuda. The severed tail section rose slowly toward the top like a wobbly bait. The now tailless fish sank nose first toward the bottom, still struggling, panic in its eyes. There its fellow barracudas closed in. The fish's body jerked as they sank wicked teeth into it.

The sea turtle did not wait to see the other barracudas tear their partner apart. It sensed the dark shadow of the boat again and moved deeper. Again it became confused. The rope around its neck held it captive no matter what it tried. The massive head had grown so large over the years it could not fit into the shell. The nylon noose could not be loosened without untieing it. If the turtle freed himself by biting it in two, it still would remain where it was. Once the loggerhead had seen a dead green turtle with such a rope still around its neck.

The large sea giant rose wearily to the surface and lay there for a moment wheezing in despair. It sucked air in gasps through wide flaring nostrils. Frosty spray flew out when it exhaled. The turtle circled aimlessly now, trying to dive. But it was unable to do so.

It hated the nearness of the boat and the people. They had come along on this calm day and turned it into a time of confusion and pain. Weariness and terror were in the turtle's body. The sun passed behind a small cloud in the sky. The loggerhead shivered in the sudden chill.

Suddenly its ears caught the sound of a splash in the water. It wondered if another 'cuda was foolish enough to attack. There was a motion in the water alongside its shell. Then it caught sight of a human—a brown, hard-muscled boy with a face mask—swimming toward him. Startled, the sea turtle swung its head in the boy's direction for the first time. They faced each other in the water. Then the loggerhead raised a weary flipper high and attempted to submerge once more.

But it was too late. A strong hand thrust itself beneath the upper shell alongside the thick neck. The hand exerted an upward pressure. Another pushed down on the rear portion of the shell. The boy's strong body fell across the turtle's back. It shuddered once, twice, apparently in revulsion from being touched.

The turtle swam forward more weakly now, forced to remain on the surface by two strong hands which held it up. The turtle no longer felt the rope. It felt the boy direct its movements toward the boat. The big flippers splashed spray.

The turtle sighed. Another sudden shudder ran through its weary body. Then it gave up the fight. It floated helplessly near the boat.

10

Surprised by his sudden dive into the sea, Ponce's friends in the skiff watched with excitement as he swam the short distance to the loggerhead. They saw him grab hold of the shell behind the turtle's head.

"Row the skiff over to me," Ponce sputtered, pushing up his face mask with one hand.

He still lay across the turtle's huge form. The loggerhead slapped his dangerous flippers and swung his heavy head back and forth like a snake. It was becoming aroused again. The bellowing through its open nostrils was terrifying to all except Ponce.

The situation was not new to him. The only difference was in the huge size of the turtle. He was accustomed to quick action in handling and wrestling these sea giants, and their broad backs were a familiar place to his wiry body. But he would have to be careful around this one.

His left hand still gripped the shell at the neck. The sea turtle rolled its black eyes back at him. Ponce noticed how they bulged. He knew he would have to boat this one fast over the roller so as not to hurt it. It was wheezing. He must keep the head up out of the water. First, because of the turtle's exhausted state. Secondly, because it would dive and pull him under if it got its head under the surface.

"Grab the boat!" shouted Miguel as he paddled the skiff the short distance to his friend in the water. Ponce's right hand came free from the rear of the turtle. He seized the boat's gunwale.

"Hurry. Take hold of the rope." Ponce spat out water.

The moment was a tense one as Miguel reached out and grabbed the rope which floated off beside the turtle's neck. He pulled hard and the turtle's huge shell bumped the boat's side for the first time.

"Hi," cried out Marco, hugging the bow seat where he had moved during the fight. "Take it easy!"

Ponce was still in the water and breathing as heavily as was the immense turtle beside him. Both had become exhausted in the hard fight.

"He's winded," said Ponce. "We must take him while he is quiet."

He let go his hold on the turtle and swung a bare leg over the skiff's side. Eager hands caught him and hauled him inside. His shorts hung to him like wet silk and dripped streams of water into the bottom where it lay in pools. He removed his face mask and tossed it onto the seat.

"What do we do now?" asked Miguel, still holding the rope tightly in both hands to keep the turtle close to the skiff.

Ponce's other friends were peering over the side at the huge back. Not Miguel. He held on with a firm grip to keep the turtle on top. Thankfully the turtle lay quietly alongside them on top and unable to move. He sucked in air and his eyes still bulged dangerously.

To make the boat safer Jorge moved ahead toward Marco in the bow. It was a smart move because it helped to balance the boat. Ponce and Miguel were both on the same side where the turtle lay. The skiff sank lower on that side with their weight and the size of the turtle, which put a stress on the rope still tight over the side.

Occasionally the loggerhead would lift its head out of the water and hiss at them. The sound was like compressed steam rushing out of a deep cavern. The intake of air was more of a sigh. The outlet was a loud hissing sound. It showed displeasure, Ponce knew. The boy swung quickly into action.

"Jorge. Miguel." Ponce moved and spoke at the same time. "Help me load him into the boat."

Ponce looked around him, glancing at Marco in the bow. That was the best place for him. He motioned for the others to move nearer to him in the middle.

"Stay here," he cautioned. "I will hand you the rope."

They were happy to stay forward, for they knew the turtle must come in over the stern on the roller like a wet and heavy net.

Now Ponce moved toward the stern. He seized the frayed rope and swung the turtle around toward the roller. The large beast towed rather easily on top of the water. When Ponce had it behind the boat he tossed the rope to the three boys up front.

"Pull hard," he shouted. "If he rests more he will fight us."

The three boys pulled hard on the rope. This moved the turtle's body in to the stern. Ponce leaned out and lifted one of the huge flippers over the roller. The boys pulled. Then he lifted the other flipper as the front shell came onto the low roller. Ahead of the turtle lay the open boat.

Ponce realized they were in a most dangerous position now. He stood all alone at the side of the turtle's head and beak. The beak could swing around and snap onto his leg if he didn't move quickly. Also, the flippers were flapping wildly and making a loud splash and noise. They might break the roller. Then they would lose the turtle for sure.

As the turtle struggled, Ponce let go the flippers and seized the rope. He threw his weight against it. Everyone pulled with all their strength. Even little Marco. The sea turtle, hissing and slapping its huge flippers, moved ahead. Ponce noticed that the actions of the turtle helped move it into the boat. The stern sank under the four hundred pounds. But it did not go under. Ponce was pleased.

"Everyone pull," he called out. He moved backward a few steps.

The bow had now risen higher into the air. Marco was farthest in the air and Jorge and Miguel next. Then came Ponce more or less now in the center of the boat. The huge turtle lay half in, half outside.

As the turtle realized its predicament, it lashed out in a fury of excitement. It began beating its flippers more wildly. Each beat was a wicked blow which shook the boat. The blows were beginning to tear the boat to pieces. A section of the inner railing flew off into the water. The rear seat had cracked.

"We will sink," Miguel cried out.

Ponce, acting like lightning, moved inside the taut rope nearer to the turtle's swaying head. He approached it and seized the big shell. His weight and that of the turtle was too much for the nineteen foot boat. Water began to pour over into the skiff. It frothed at his feet.

"Jorge. Miguel! " yelled Ponce. His friends on the rope stared at Ponce. "Move toward the bow," Ponce shouted.

But as he said it he saw that by the boat's angle and the fact they could not let go of the tight rope, it was hopeless. If they did the turtle might slip off the stern into the sea and be lost.

It was Marco who acted. He backed as far as he could out over the high bow, holding on with both hands and feet like a monkey. He was so far out that most of his body was out of the boat. Ponce could only see his head.

Marco's quick action, as the others strained at the rope, raised the stern several inches. As it did the turtle moved forward with the boated water that held some of his weight. Ponce reached beneath the turtle's front shell and seized soft flesh. His hands closed hard on it. He got hold of rough, pliable skin. The loggerhead had a strong smell like wet fish. Then Ponce pulled hard, putting his entire body into it.

The turtle came aboard the boat with a splash and thorough confusion. It slid right by Ponce, who fell and lay on his back in the water on the boat's floorboards. The turtle went by him and lodged partly under a center seat. It slid like a pancake and could not flap its flippers at all. The motion of the water sliding forward, the boat changing position, and Ponce's weight falling forward had all worked to assist in the capture.

Miguel and Jorge lost their balance and fell into the boat almost on top of the turtle. And Marco fell out. He lost his grip on the bow and splashed into the sea.

Ponce leaped quickly onto his feet. He reached outside and grabbed Marco's hair and held him up alongside the boat. Then the three of them hauled their scared friend aboard before the barracudas could get to him. Marco lay in a heap like the turtle inside the boat, wet and frightened.

They all slapped him on his wet shoulders. He had done it. Little Marco was a hero. His quick action had changed the entire fight to boat the turtle. It had cost him a dunking, but it was worth it.

The turtle hissed fearfully beneath the seat. Its back was in open view, lodged between the center seat and the stern. But the head and part of its shell were lodged under the seat.

Ponce stood up, his chest heaving for grabs of air. He had fought hard and had won. The boat would hold them all. He watched the birds leave them and fly off.

"He is ours," he said. "He is the biggest I have ever seen!"

Then his body sank to a still intact seat to rest.

This one will take different handling. I wonder if he can be taught? He is so wise and so old in years. It will not be easy. Maybe my father is right. This is a dangerous life.

It was a day unlike any other day he had known. Now they must return and put the turtle into the pens. He smiled as he saw his tired friends lying inside the boat. Relief swept over his body. They had stuck with him and had proved they had courage.

It was a day Ponce would long remember.

A brave tern flew over them, head down, piping shrill cries at the huge turtle. Its wings beat faster than the eye could see. It was white with a black patch on its head. Its beak was orange. It was a beautiful sight for them all to see.

11

The boys retraced their path back into the harbor. The white brick lighthouse loomed over them, rising high above a cluster of coconut palms. They rode the incoming tide swiftly, taking full advantage of its flood.

As they swept past anchored yachts in the harbor, people rushed on deck to wave at the brave crew. They passed some local fishermen on the shoreline handling long cane poles. These men fished for grunts, jacks, grouper, and small snapper from the seawall. They waved.

Ponce and Miguel rowed side by side coming in. The turtle was still lodged under the seat, but now and then banged its head as it raised it. Marco and Jorge sat up forward.

Ponce's muscled back bent strongly to an oar. He and Miguel worked in close harmony at the sweeps. It was now merely a matter of keeping the boat straight in the strong current. The turtle had made the boat much heavier. It sank low in the water. Thus, the tide did most of the hard work for them.

Ponce was in a gay mood. He smiled back at the waving people and called out aloud to those fishermen he recognized on the shore. Some of them realized Ponce had caught another sea turtle to wrestle. Nothing was very secret in Key West, which was like all small American towns. They were glad for the boy. They admired his strength, skill and courage. It also made Ponce feel very big inside. Today he felt pride in his work.

The laden skiff swept past more boats where curious persons in colorful shirts and shorts rushed to the rails to see what the four boys had caught. Their mouths flew open when they saw the giant turtle wedged on the floor. Many of them had never seen a sea turtle.

"Oh—what a monster," they called out. Some women wore red blouses and white shorts or slacks. These were tourists, Ponce observed, and not very wise about the ways of his life.

"Say, he's a giant," one man said. "How did you ever catch such a big one?"

Then the small boat was swept from their view as the turtle wrestler approached a new future. Ponce knew this giant loggerhead would lure many tourists into the pens. He would be responsible for them coming. It might mean favor in his father's eyes. That would make him as happy as he was now bringing in the turtle.

Finally, they drew alongside the dock from which they had left earlier that same day. Ponce tossed the bow line to the boards overhead and quickly scrambled up to tie it. The bow of the old skiff rubbed the pilings gratefully. Then it lay still in the slack.

Miguel, Jorge, and Marco followed Ponce to the dock. They looked down and saw now why their arrival had caused so much enthusiasm along the waterfront. The loggerhead looked tremendous in the boat. Seeing it now, they all wondered how they had managed.

Ponce spoke to them: "We must pick up some fresh fish to feed the turtle," he said. "We will go first to Placido's and get some fish heads and insides."

"Why the fish shop?" asked Miguel curiously.

"Waggle makes me feed my own turtle," replied Ponce. "It's our agreement." He reflected on the deal. The shrewd owner had to feed the other turtles. Why not Ponce's? He shrugged. It was Waggle's way. And the fish heads cost nothing.

"We'll go with you," Marco said. None of the boys had any desire to remain with the boat now that their feet were again on land, or at least on a dock, jutting out from the land. Ponce studied them and realized this. He flashed a white smile. They would all go and none would be responsible in case the turtle acted up. It was very much in their minds, he knew.

"The turtle will be safe here," Ponce said. He noticed the signs of relief cross their faces. "He can't get out of the boat and it is much too large for him to tip. We will put some heavy concrete blocks in the bow to raise the stern higher. That's all."

He asked Marco and Jorge to get the blocks. They ran toward the shore where they soon found several cast up on the rocky shoreline. Together they picked them up.

While they were gone Miguel asked Ponce a question that had been bothering him. "I have often wondered why fishermen turn turtles on their backs when they catch them in the big boats? Why is that?"

Ponce sat down alongside Miguel. "A sea turtle can't turn over once he's been turned upside down," he explained. "They can be shipped easier in this manner.

Also many Indians in the lands of Costa Rica and Nicaraugua turn them onto their backs on the beaches. This is illegal, because they are nesting. But they do it."

"It's against the law, I know," replied Miguel.

"Many things are against the law," Ponce observed wisely. "But some people think the law is for others. Not themselves."

"That is true," Miguel agreed. Ponce continued:

"I know of a man who did this thing once. He and his friends caught and butchered a sea turtle on the beach and cooked it over a fire. The next day he was sorry about it. He was sorry the rest of his life and joined a group that raises young sea turtles to release them in the sea."

"Nature is very interesting," added Miguel. He paused and looked keenly at his young friend. "I'd like to know as much about life as you do, Ponce."

"I know very little about life," Ponce replied seriously. "Ask the man who killed the turtle and now raises them. He knows more. It is a very deep thing, this living. I'm mixed up sometimes about it." He shook his black hair and grinned at Miguel.

He studied the open sea off the dock. It was bathed in the strong light of a clear day. He thought of Mr. Foster at the aquarium who was always puttering around his tanks and doing scientific experiments in his laboratory. He had a kind word for everyone. His blue eyes always sparkled behind rimless spectacles when he talked. He was always busy, if very forgetful.

Ponce felt Mr. Foster knew about life. So did his own father. And Cliff Waggle. Everyone it seemed, except Ponce. They each had set a course in life. Only he was drifting aimlessly.

Miguel was silent, knowing of Ponce's problem. "Let's

go to Placido's," said Ponce. "Marco and Jorge can toss the blocks in the boat."

Miguel struggled to his feet. Ponce was striding off the dock. He ran to catch up.

12

They turned right at the first street that ran parallel to the winding waterfront and then went two blocks inland from where they had tied the skiff. Marco and Jorge soon joined them and they all walked closely together, brown legs flashing like shears. They laughed and joked in the joy of being ashore after such a hard and dangerous trip to sea. Jorge had put his brown leather sandals back on his feet and his guide cap was perched jauntily on his head. He kicked at an empty tin can in the street.

The elderly Cubans sitting in the shade of the buildings along the hot waterfront streets looked up as the small merry group passed. They imagined this carefree band was headed for the baseball diamond. They saw Marco's red cap. Little did they know of the sea adventure. The buildings threw some shade onto the pavement. They stood and sat in the shade, not seeking the sun as the boys did. They envied the boys' joy in life.

Some dogs sat in the dust and kicked fleas on their necks with their hind legs. Nearly every store the boys passed had loud music blaring from inside. The stores smelled of tobacco and chicory-laden Cuban coffee. It was a good place, Ponce thought. The homes were white and clean and mostly on two levels. They had front porches and upstairs balconies. Some even had widow's walks atop their roofs.

Placido's "Red Snapper" fish shop was recognizable to any customers looking for it by the enormous sign he had hung out over his front door. It had a large and crudely drawn red snapper with huge goggle eyes made out of green reflecting beads so they would glow at night. The sign itself was cut into the shape of a fish and at night it looked real with the eyes glowing. Many persons had stopped, stared, and hurried on. It was very weird at night. Supernatural, some said.

It didn't take the noisy little group long to reach Placido's screened door. They entered. They noticed Placido was busy with several customers. The people in the shop turned to look curiously at the small band which had burst in unexpectedly. Placido glanced over his spectacles at them sharply. He pursed his lips. Quiet—he was saying to them in sign language.

He continued waiting on his cash customers. He knew Ponce was after fish heads and would pay him nothing. He did not care. It saved him the trouble of carrying them out to the trash cans back in the alley.

Ponce noticed that Placido looked over toward him on several occasions and began whispering to his customers. In turn they turned to stare at the brown boy in the red shorts. Some of them left the store with a smile at Ponce and his friends. They departed hurriedly for home with their wet, cool fishes tied up in newspapers under their arms.

When they had all gone, Placido, in a long white apron covered with fresh fish scales turned to them, asking: "What brings you today?" It was the usual question. He already knew the answer. "With such a racket too!" He frowned at them.

"We want some fish for my turtle," proudly explained Ponce.

"Aiye?" Ponce saw Placido's brows raise with the question.

"I caught a new one," the boy explained. "It is hungry."

"I know," said Placido. "In fact I was telling my customers. Is it as big as I have heard?" News traveled fast in Key West.

"Yes," replied Ponce as Placido dug into the fish box to produce some chopped fish parts. As Ponce explained about the turtle Placido stuffed a small cardboard box full of the heads and leftovers from his knife. He shook his head from side to side. It was a long story to hear. He listened paitently.

Meanwhile, unknown to Ponce and his friends in the fish shop, the skiff they had left with turtle had drifted away from the dock. The bow line had come loose from the cleat which held it. Possibly it had weakened in the fray with the turtle. In any event, the skiff moved a vew feet away and a puff of wind turned it slightly. Without any direction at first, the boat spun in crazy circles as it drifted along with the tide. No one nearby had noticed.

The boat had already bumped into the pilings of one dock as the stern swung wide. Then it had floated free again and was swept along with the current. In this crazy dance across the water it had bounced from pier to pier until it came to rest near a weather-beaten dock which looked just like any in Key West.

This dock was only a few blocks away from the Turtle Pens and the cannery. Several boats were berthed alongside this dock. Of all the places the boat could have finally drifted with its live cargo, this was the worst spot in all of the city. It was a commercial fishing dock and the boats were shrimpers. They had their nets strung up to dry.

The tiny skiff and the loggerhead banged into a boat. A scurrying of feet was heard inside. Someone knocked over a tin pan. A yell and then silence. Someone was coming up topside to see what this banging was about.

To make it worse, no commercial fisherman was above picking up a stray sea turtle as a gift. Even a tough loggerhead.

13

The boat which the skiff had banged into had the name *Sea Queen* painted on its stern.

"Why can't that tide run one way for six hours straight?" complained Pablo, a dark-skinned man who stuck his black curly head through the hatch. He emerged on deck, barefooted, and went aft. He wondered about the noise he had heard below.

Pablo was a black-bearded shrimp fisherman who looked like a pirate. He wore a small black beret on his head and had on a horizontally striped red and white polo shirt. Pablo rarely wore shoes. The exception was on Saturday nights when he went to town to have some fun and buy tobacco. Then he gave in and donned a pair of low-cut, white tennis shoes with the front of the toes cut out. He always cut out the toes in his shoes to give his feet some air.

When he observed the huge loggerhead in the floating skiff below his mouth popped open, showing his white teeth for an instant above his beard. He stood motionless trying to figure out this miracle. His black eyes darted to the turtle with a slyness that made them sparkle. He studied the drifting boat, the frayed line, and the turtle. With a quick glance toward the cannery to make sure no one was watching him, Pablo leaned over and dragged the skiff's painter onto the *Sea Queen.*

"Ah—what a fine turkle!"

The beret-topped seaman muttered beneath his breath prayers for this gift from the sea as he worked the skiff toward the port side of his boat. It could not be seen there hidden between boat and dock. It was a perfect place to work without any prying eyes.

"It is a gift from the saints," he muttered again.

His hands worked quickly. Years at sea alone made Pablo talk to himself. He was a crafty man, always ready to make an easy dollar and preferring it to hard work. Sometimes he chartered his boat to deep-sea treasure hunters and lay on deck while they worked over the side with their air tanks and goggles. Trawling for shrimp was a hard night's work. Usually Pablo shrimped only when he had to. He owned his boat and was beholden to no one.

Pablo had the skiff trussed alongside in a twinkling. He leaped catlike to the topside of a covered hatch on the *Sea Queen*'s deck and seized a rope dangling from the boom. On the far end was a pulley. Through this pulley ran the heavy rope.

Within a minute he had the rope and boom swung over the floating skiff. Holding the loose end of the rope, he leaped down into the skiff and made his way to the loggerhead. Then he began to run the rope over and under its body. Shortly the big sea creature was trussed up. He tied the rope in a firm knot across the turtle's back, patted it, and climbed back into his shrimper.

Pablo leaned on the rail and looked about. By all visible signs it appeared that he had not been watched. The clanking noises down at the pens still sounded busy and undisturbed. No fisherman from the shore had observed his actions.

Pablo grabbed the other end of the rope that hung down through the pulley. He walked to a small deck winch and coiled it around the capstan. Then he started the engine. The rope caught and the loggerhead was slowly raised up out of the skiff.

When he had hoisted the turtle a foot higher than the rail, Pablo ran quickly along the deck. The boom swung wildly with the turtle swaying in mid air and hissing in rage. Pablo now eased off on the winch and lowered the heavy load to the deck. It thumped to the planks and lay in the cool shadow cast by the high rail. There the turtle rested, working its wet eyes in alarm.

Pablo worked quickly. He shut off the winch motor and untied the rope from around the loggerhead. The turtle bellowed madly at him. Pablo seized the shell on one side. Then he threw his body into the effort and flipped the turtle onto its broad back. He ran to a hose and sprayed the sea turtle to cool it down. Then he seized a piece of brown canvas and tossed it over his prize catch.

Pablo sank down weakly onto a hatch and stroked his black beard. His eyes gleamed at the thought of the profit this turtle would bring him at the turtle cannery. It wasn't as valuable as a green turtle, but it could be made into soup. He stroked his beard and figured. The money could keep him tied up at his dock for another month. He rose and made a barefooted crossing of the wet deck.

Pablo's nimble hands untied the skiff's painter and he gave it a yank forward. Then he towed it to the stern of his boat and cast the rope loose. The skiff swirled and turned around. It drifted off.

Pablo crossed the *Sea Queen* again and made his way toward the bow of his boat. He untied the forward line holding the shrimp boat to the dock. Then he made his way to the stern and loosened another line. As the craft floated free he went to the stern and pushed a button in the wheelhouse. The engine below decks started with a cough. He backed out into the tide and swung toward the Turtle Pens.

The dumpy *Sea Queen* with its rust-streaked sides chugged its way to the outer T-shaped dock of the pens, where Pablo silenced his engine. A few sweating men on the dock helped him tie up. They knew Pablo well because he was a fisherman of some talents who often brought in a turtle for them. Today they called out to him.

"What is it today, Pablo? Another *turkle?*" They laughed as they mimicked his odd manner of speech.

But Pablo ignored them. He realized the less he said the better. His liking for an occasional easy dollar was well known to the men at the pens.

"Just tie me up, amigos. Then look under the canvas." This said, Pablo scrambled along the deck and flipped back the canvas hiding the loggerhead. "Is it not a giant?" He spoke in pride. The turtle men stared at the big sea turtle with experienced eyes.

"But Pablo. It is only a loggerhead," said one. "It is only good for the the soup making. The meat is too tough."

"It will not bring much money," cautioned another man who wore a rubber apron. He knew Pablo would dicker with them. The black apron covered a bare chest and hung to his knees. His body was covered with black, wiry hair. It

crossed Pablo's mind that he looked much like an ape.
"Never mind," said Pablo. "It is worth something. Haul
it out of here." He grinned toothily from his black beard.
The men were always full of jokes. Today he did not mind.
It was a lucky day.

Using Pablo's boom they hauled the turtle up and over
to the dock. There they loosened the ropes holding him.
Spraying the dock with water to wet it down ahead of
him, two of the barefooted men slid the loggerhead toward
the cannery doors. It was true, as Pablo said. It was a very
large turtle and worth something as soup. They did not
toss it into the pens below with the green turtles. They
were afraid it would attack them. It would be better to
slaughter it quickly.

"Where did you get it, Pablo?" inquired one of the
turtle men.

Pablo shot him a sharp, sidelong glance from beneath his
beret. Had one of them seen him steal the turtle? He
shoved his beret back on his head. His beard stuck out
defiantly.

"Wall, you see, it just drifted along into my boat," he
said. "It was there all alone so I just picked it up." He
watched their reactions to this statement of truth. He
especially watched the man who had spoken to him last.
There was no indication on his face that he had seen
anything going on at the dock.

At this remark the men laughed loudly. "You are a
funny one, Pablo," one said. "Always making with the
jokes."

They all knew that Pablo fished hard when he worked.
And he was not above making them think he did not have
to work very hard. They thought the matter a joke.

"Is it your birthday?" they asked. "Maybe it was a gift."

74

"Did he climb into the boat on his own?"

"Maybe he stole it. Call the police!"

Pablo surveyed them haughtily. "Pay me," he said. "And be quick about it seeing you have just hauled my turtle off."

He hated the delay. Something might go wrong. Someone might even appear to claim the turtle. He wanted to get the matter settled quickly.

"It is worth only fifty dollars," said another seaman who walked toward the shrimper from the darkened interior of the cannery building. "At that we are being very generous.

"It is worth seventy-five dollars." Pablo lighted his pipe.

"We might offer sixty five." Pablo pondered this new offer. The pipe made gurgling sounds.

"I'll take it," he said.

Thus Pablo was paid off in cash for his sudden good fortune. That morning he had less than a dollar in change in his pockets. Now he had sixty five dollars bound up with a rubber band. Pablo decided to get off the dock. He would not have to shrimp for more than a month.

The turtle had disappeared into the cannery, where it had been weighed on a floor scale. Here its fate was being decided while they wet it down with a hose. Pablo pushed his boat away from the slippery pier while hearing the bellowing inside the slaughterhouse.

It was a short trip to his dock. He tied up and dashed below to find his open-toed sneakers. He was going downtown.

He would not see the loggerhead again. Nor for long some of the money that lay so heavily in his right hand pocket.

14

When Ponce and his friends returned to the dock they discovered the skiff gone. Their hearts sank at the sight of the empty space.

Ponce immediately noticed that the rope had become undone and realized that the weight of the turtle had been too much strain on it. The skiff had drifted somewhere with the tide. His eyes searched in that direction at once.

Miguel looked sadly at Ponce. "It is gone," he said. "What will we do?"

He was as discouraged as the others. Marco and Jorge looked stunned. All began to search the harbor with their sharp eyes. It was no good. The skiff had disappeared.

Ponce still held the box of wet fish. With sinking heart, he told them, "We must find the skiff."

"We couldn't catch another turtle like that in a hundred years, I'll bet," volunteered Marco.

"No," replied Ponce sadly.

"We will all help," Jorge said. "I can go to one dock. Marco to another. We'll all scatter. One of us will find the skiff and the turtle."

Ponce agreed to the plan. The tide, he knew, would have taken the boat toward the Turtle Pens. He told them this and pointed in that direction. "Each of you take a different dock and search among the boats for the skiff," he said. "It may have lodged among some big shrimp boats. I will go directly to the pens and look. They know me there and can help."

The boys were cheered by the prospect of another hunt for the turtle. At first, they had felt sick in their stomachs when they found the dock empty. But now they had a task to do, and they each scattered in the general direction of the Turtle Pens and cannery. Their spirits went from low despair to high enthusiasm. It was a game to them to hunt. Only Ponce felt low in spirit.

"Join me at the pens," Ponce called as they fled the dock. He walked toward shore and turned left. He was hoping one of them would find the skiff alongside a dock where it could not be seen from where they had stood. It had to be somewhere.

Ponce reached the pens and entered the courtyard. He walked past everyone and went directly to the cannery. The men inside saw him coming and stopped their work. They respected the young boy and often stopped their work to watch him wrestle in the water. Ponce glared around the room of death. Their was no warmness here.

The sweating men were bare from the waist up. Their pallid bodies beside his brown one gleamed with perspiration as they worked in the heat of steam rising from large copper-coated kettles. Many turtles lay in the cannery slaughterhouse since the ship had unloaded. Most had gone into the pens, but some were needed for soup and turtle steak. All were on their backs, wet and softly sighing their odd sounds.

"Hi, Ponce," called out a youngish man, wiping his

77

brow. He had a long moustache which hung down each side of his mouth.

"How's sponging?" asked another, his belly hanging over his pants belt.

"Want to buy a big turtle?" One leaned on an axe.

The men all laughed at this. They knew that Ponce had lost his loggerhead but hadn't heard he had been out hunting for another. Ponce ignored their crude jokes. He glanced around the room by habit. His eyes were getting more accustomed to the dim interior.

"I might want to buy a turtle. But it has to be big," he said.

He studied each man as he said this. He was seeking clues. Anything. It might lead to something one of them knew. The men grinned. They had not expected Ponce to say he'd buy a turtle. He did not have that much money they knew. Ponce never bought turtles.

To Ponce's nose the slaughterhouse was damp and reeked with the strange fishy smell of many turtles. The floor was concrete and wet with water and streaks of blood. It made Ponce sick to his stomach to come inside. He didn't like the slaughterhouse and actually never came near it when he wrestled outside. He hated it.

Ponce spoke louder: "I say again. I would buy a turtle if you had one big enough. I don't want little green ones. Not like these." He gave one a kick with his bare foot.

"Maybe we have," said one of the workmen. "Just how big?"

"Four hundred." replied Ponce. He was interested in the way the talk was going. Although the men were using him for diversion, he felt an electricity in the room. They knew something they were holding back. This was their manner of joking. They would spring it on him when they were ready.

They were strange, silent men, much like hangmen.

78

They spoke little and made friends with no one. Cliff Waggle walked suddenly into the slaughterhouse.

"What's this about buying a turtle?"

Two men, each stripped to the waist and hairy chested, came into the butchering room dragging a large turtle behind them on its back. They had tied a rope behind the hind flippers to move it along the slick floor. It was a huge turtle, Ponce noted. And a loggerhead.

"Ponce wants to buy a turtle to wrestle in the pens, seeing he is out of one to wrestle right now," confided a man who seemed the boss of the workmen. He chomped on a big black looking cigar. He wore a striped shirt and gray pants.

Ponce began to study the turtle, not the man. He noticed how closely this turtle resembled the big one he and his crew had captured at sea only this morning. He studied the big yellow scaly head, the protruding eyes, and the flippers without holes. Its shell looked enormous even when turned upside down in the shed.

He watched as they prepared the turtle for butchering. A thin man with his pants rolled up to his knees picked up a running hose and sprayed the turtle from head to tail. The water cleaned it thoroughly. Then he kicked the loggerhead around with his bare feet until its head lay across a low wooden timber bolted to the floor. But the loggerhead rebelled at this. It hissed and bellowed. The cannery room shook with violence. The angry turtle raised its shell partly off the floor in an effort to escape the axe.

All at once it came to Ponce. This *was* his turtle. He was not looking at a duplicate. This was the big loggerhead. He could tell by its spirit as well as its size. It was his. The old one.

Ponce stepped forward. "Maybe I won't have to buy today," he said.

He examined the turtle closely, holding back the thin man with the upraised axe. He glanced up at Cliff Waggle from beside the turtle. "Look here," he challenged all of them.

Waggle strode over to the loggerhead. His red face appeared more blotchy than usual from the inside heat. He did not know what Ponce was leading up to, but the turtle represented a lot of money to him. He scratched under his armpit.

Ponce had noticed a detail none of the men had seen. The turtle's eyes searched his own almost knowingly. It was the same sad look he had noticed at sea when it had given up the fight.

"This turtle is mine," he argued. The turtle was only an axe blow away from death. Ponce had to impress Waggle now. So much hung on it.

The cannery boss in the striped shirt clamped down hard on his cigar. He looked Ponce over slyly. He noticed the thin, hard, razor keen brown body. He meant everything he said, and the cannery boss believed that Ponce actually meant to take this turtle away from him. He had paid Pablo sixty five dollars for it out of Waggle's money. He paled at the thought of what his boss would do if he had made a mistake.

"Prove it," the cannery boss said. "Pablo sold us the turtle only today. He brought it to us."

He glanced up wisely at Waggle. The men stood around not knowing whether to work or not. They did not know how Waggle would take this. Even from Ponce.

"Look here," said Ponce. He bent down alongside the turtle and picked up its front flipper. He held it out. "What do you see?" he asked them all.

The men looked at the turtle's flipper and then glanced

back at their boss. The cannery boss rubbed his chin and stroked an imaginary beard. He did not know what Ponce was driving at. He wished he knew. Maybe the turtle had some initials marked on it.

Then Ponce said: "This turtle bears no capture marks, no holes in any of his flippers. Nor are there any holes in the rear of his shell. How is Pablo, a fisher of the nets, going to catch such a turtle? Only by spearing or tieing it on deck with the ropes through the flippers."

Waggle bent down closer to look at all flippers. The turtle did not have any marks on it, as Ponce had pointed out. He stood up straight looking hard across the room. The men stood silent, waiting. The dank air of the cannery grew silent.

"Where did Pablo get it?" Waggle asked tersely.

"He would not tell us, but joked about it," said the man in the striped shirt. Suddenly he remembered. "Pablo said he found the turtle, that it drifted into his boat."

The men suddenly laughed at him. He paled. Pablo had sold it fairly.

Ponce continued to push his advantage.

"Pablo did not know it was my turtle. He found it in my boat which drifted free from my dock. He told you the truth. And you were tricked."

Waggle listened without comment while the boy explained how he and his friends had gone out in the skiff and fought the big turtle until they captured it. He told Waggle of the troubles they had boating it. Then he explained how they had tied the boat to the dock and gone for some fish. The boat had drifted away. It was not their fault.

"Come," said Cliff Waggle abruptly. Then, turning to his men, He said: "Do not butcher this turtle. Put it aside."

They obeyed as he left with Ponce. They slid the turtle into a wet corner of the shed. The air had become less tense inside the room.

When they entered his office located at the far end of the gift shop, Waggle walked over to his desk and began to thumb absently through some papers. He soon found one signed by Pablo. It was a receipt for the loggerhead.

The green paper was all proper and legal looking. Ponce felt weak inside. It was the law, something he had always respected. It was written convincingly in black and white on the paper. A paper held power. Yet Ponce knew that the loggerhead was his.

"This is it," muttered Waggle. "Sixty five dollars for a tough soup turtle. My, oh my, oh my." He began scratching behind his ear.

"Your men bought a stolen turtle," Ponce argued. "Is there no justice in the law?"

"Well, now," replied Cliff Waggle. "There is and there ain't. It is all the way a man looks at it. The turtle actually is mine due to this receipt. I can do what I want with it since I bought it fairly. This is the law!"

Waggle studied the boy standing stiffly in front of him. Ponce looked weary from his long day at sea. Waggle realized both had told the truth about this strange turtle. Neither Ponce nor Pablo had lied.

So Ponce had really caught a big turtle after all, Waggle thought. He must tell Captain Anderson about this!

There was a timid knock at the office door. "Come in," said Waggle.

Miguel entered, followed closely by Jorge and Marco. They were still breathless from running. "We heard you found the turtle," said Miguel. "How did it get here?"

Waggle grunted and coughed. "Ask a crooked old shrimper," he said. Then in a less severe tone, he added:

82

"This turtle must be a hundred years old, Ponce. I seriously doubt it would make good soup. I am thinking of getting it off my hands. If yew want to wrestle it in the pens it is all yours. I shall give it back."

Ponce looked up at Waggle, relieved. "But about Pablo?"

"Pablo does not matter."

"But he *took* the sixty-five dollars!"

"Pablo will learn someday that he owes me for a turtle. Just how I can not tell now. It won't be to his liking, nor will he know when. I have ways."

A smile lit up Waggle's reddish face. It was a secretive, rare burst of inner feeling. Somehow Waggle relished the thought of coming to grips with the shrimper, Pablo. Ponce felt he knew now who would win. Yankee ingenuity would not be lacking in the battle of wits over the price of the turtle.

A feeling of happiness swept over Ponce. Marco picked up the box with the fish heads. His red baseball cap was perched sideways on his head. This made him look ridiculous since the peak stuck out over one ear. Ponce laughed at Marco's appearance. He felt good about how all his friends had helped him this day.

"Thank you, Mr. Waggle," he said to the owner of the Turtle Pens.

"It will be good for wrestling," Waggle answered. Then, after a pause: "I just hope you can handle this one. The turtle is very large and old. He will be very set in his ways. And wise."

"I will tame him first," replied Ponce.

"Yes, admitted Waggle with a shrug of his heavy shoulders. "The loggerhead will need lots of training. If we put him in the larger pen with the greens he will fight them." He studied Ponce carefully. "Have yew ever considered he might break loose from the usual small pen? It is not as strong as the larger ones."

"He is not *that* fierce," the boy replied.

"I saw a look in his old eyes. I wonder." Waggle admired Ponce's good sense and vitality. But he realized the boy was overeager now. Having recovered his turtle had stimulated him.

The small group left the office and went outside to the docks. Waggle ordered the men in the cannery to bring the turtle outside and put it in Ponce's small training pen. The men did and lowered it by a thick rope net that fitted beneath its body. Into the net's sides hooks were placed and the whole affair lifted into the air by an overhead boom and pulley through which a rope ran to the net.

When the loggerhead struck the water with a splash he struggled free of the heavy net and swam strongly ahead. He hit the wire side along the bay. It bulged a little. But it held and kept him enclosed. Ponce watched the turtle turn and ram the other side. It was solid steel. His head took the blow and it made his neck recoil. He backed off, then dived to the bottom.

"He doesn't take too well to confinement," said Waggle, observing the obvious. They had all noticed this.

"I will master him," came the almost inaudible reply from the brown boy at his shoulder.

Waggle shook his head from side to side. "Or he—you!"

Waggle continued to shake his head as he walked back toward his office. He must go find Captain Anderson now and tell him about this latest yarn about Ponce. He wanted to see his face when he told him about the big turtle the boy had caught with three friends in a boat the size of one of the *Andy Hank*'s dories. He chuckled to himself as he walked into his office and grabbed the phone.

84

15

Ponce awoke the next day an hour before the Turtle Pens opened for business. He dressed quietly, not waking his father, knowing it was time to begin to tame the sea turtle. He closed the front door and walked down the street lined with garbage cans and stray cats. A fresh breeze moved in from the bay.

At the pens he walked through the front and entered the gift shop where he found Sally Barlow dusting the curios with a dilapidated turkey feather duster. It must have been an heirloom from her attic. Ponce smiled.

As she noticed him enter, Sally said: "What brings you out so early? I heard you had a real busy day yesterday. What with the aquarium tanks and the sea turtle." Swish, swish went the duster.

Ponce felt the early morning cool air move like a dampness through the shop. The only noise in there Sally made, walking around the various cases. He liked the gift shop when it did not have any people in it. The confusion of the hordes of tourists and the humid heat of the day made it much different. He liked the mornings alone with Sally.

Many of the large conch shells were made into lamps. They were lighted inside by small electric bulbs. He liked the shells and their lights. He had brought the shells in from the reef and thought he recognized every one. Especially the helmet conchs. They were shaped like a conquistador's metal helmet and were valuable. They shone brilliantly. This part of the shop really was due to his efforts. It gave him a twinge of satisfaction. It was the same at the aquarium. He had stocked it too with shells and sponges.

He jarred himself back to the living. Ponce glanced at Sally and said: "Sorry. I just came to work with the turtle a bit." He did not mean to be rude. He had been thinking about his own life.

"What happened at the aquarium can happen again," warned Sally. That old Mr. Foster is too wrapped up in his science. He is wide open for trouble, I think!" she snorted. Then suddenly she sneezed. The dust settled.

Ponce delayed his trip outside to the pens. He started to ask her why she felt something else would happen. In his own mind he thought he knew the answer. Mr. Foster was too old, too tied up in scientific experiments, too understaffed, and too kind. Someone was evidently out to ruin his business. It might be an enemy in the Upper Keys. Or even Miami.

"I guess it will happen again," Ponce admitted. He paused to lean on the long glass showcase full of sea fans and brain coral. Even Sally had an interest in Mr. Foster. Why?

"Can you tame the new turtle?" Sally asked, changing the subject. She stopped her dusting job and faced Ponce.

She noticed his bare feet and his shorts. "It is such dangerous work. My, oh my!"

"Yes, I caught him. And sooner or later I'll tame him. It is still only a turtle!"

"He seems so much different from the rest," Sally confided. "After I was through working yesterday I watched him for awhile in the pen. He is restless, Ponce. He wants his freedom very badly."

"My good upbringing will win out."

"Shoosh—you crazy!" Sally said.

"He will bring many tourists. They buy your sea shells," Ponce added.

"You could get hurt too."

Ponce quit kidding. He remained silent. He liked Sally. Something drew him to her.

"They come anyway," Sally reminded him. "They always do."

She was thinking of her own two boys and of her husband who was killed by the falling block in the rigging. It had been lonely for her ever since. In her heart she felt Ponce was one of her boys. He often bought her boys candy and cokes after his turtle wrestling. He was their idol.

"Take care, Sally," said Ponce. "I must go to the pen and try the turtle out. Maybe he has been talking to my father. Then I won't be able to train him at all."

"Take care Ponce." Sally returned to her dusting. Her turkey duster moved faster as the boy walked out the rear door to the patio. She studied his strong body, observing his graceful walk and the way his muscles rippled under his brown skin. She hoped her boys would grow up as self-reliant as Ponce. But not wrestling turtles! "That's out," she muttered to herself. "I'd as soon get scorpion bit!"

Ponce approached the small pen which held the turtle. He leaned on the rail and watched the loggerhead swim below him. The turtle swam on top of the water with its head out. Its eyes surveyed Ponce. The boy turtle wrestler felt a thrill going over him. The turtle revealed no fear. Nor recognition. Nothing. It was a cold reptilian.

Ponce slid down into the pool from a ladder that led straight down into the enclosed pen. The turtle dived when it saw him. Deeply. It made a soft swoosh as it sucked air through its nostrils before they closed shut for the dive. The turtle's quick move only left ripples on the water where it had been a moment before. Ponce knew the loggerhead had sought the bottom of the tank. There it would hide. But it would need air. The water felt unusually cool against Ponce's body as he swam on top of the water.

He floated for awhile waiting for the turtle to come up. He knew the loggerhead would have to surface shortly. And it did. It came up on Ponce's left side across the pen. Ponce swam over to the bobbing hulk as the beast's nostrils flew open. The head reared up out of the water, the eyes searching.

With experience born from wrestling many turtles over the years, Ponce slipped up behind the turtle and ran his right hand over the barnacled shell. He tried for the handhold he liked beneath the front at the top of the neck. He had to be careful while in the water. This was no tired turtle today.

With a lunge the loggerhead broke away. Its powerful front flippers propelled its body across the tank. As it fled the loggerhead swung its head in Ponce's direction. Ponce knew the turtle was determined to keep an eye on him. It seemed very strong after a night of rest. It now fought with brute animal strength.

Two figures appeared at the railing over the pen. Ponce saw them from the water where he swam. They pointed a movie camera at him. There was a man and a woman, evidently his wife. The woman held a sharp pointed nail to her lips. Ponce knew she was worried about him. He grinned his wide white grin and the man got a closeup of Ponce with his zoom lens. That would look good at home in Kansas, he told himself.

Ponce dived now, trying to fool or confuse the turtle. He came up suddenly on the right of the leathery back. He had surprised the turtle. But the loggerhead tilted smoothly and escaped from his slippery grasp. It turned sideways to avoid the boy. This turtle has learned much, Ponce admitted. It was using its natural cunning and skill against him. It had not become sluggish with age. The boy wrestler blew out water and surveyed the situation.

After an hour Ponce gave up. He hauled himself up the ladder dripping wet to the dock. There he sat down in a pool of water while the sun worked on his goose pimples. He thought it over. The turtle again sounded, invisible now in the silted bay water. Ponce recalled how he had put his hands on the loggerhead several times and then lost him. He is terribly strong and smart, he admitted to himself. He has the instincts of all wild things. Maybe he will out-wit me.

More tourists had collected around the boy. All had cameras and snapped pictures of him. A stocky attendant walked up. It was Charley King, who fed the green turtles. He was old and had a grizzled salt and pepper beard. He wore a yellow sport shirt with blue pants. The shirt had a "TURTLE PENS" patch on the sleeve.

"Throw him some balao today, Charley. I want him to eat well. Tomorrow I will try it again."

"You did not ride him I see." From a distance Charley

King had observed the struggle between Ponce and the sea turtle.

"No—I could not hold him. He is very swift and smart. I am learning to respect him more. He does not tame easily." The old man's eyes lighted up with strange fires and faded just as old fires burn out quickly. He shuffled off.

"I will feed him some squid I have," he said. "Old turtles like fresh squid."

"Thank you," said Ponce. He leaped to his feet and left the pens for the day.

16

On his way home for lunch Ponce turned in the direction of the Oceanic Aquarium. Last night he had thought a great deal about Mr. Foster and the odd manner in which he operated his business. It could be run more efficiently, Ponce knew. Then he asked himself out loud why it had to be *him* Mr. Foster needed. Why Ponce? His mind was on the fish tanks as well as his rebellion. He walked quickly to see how the fish had made out overnight.

Ponce walked through the open ray mouth of the aquarium and entered the lobby. This was a spot he liked every time he came to the aquarium. The lobby, although starkly plain, had a large skylight overhead that allowed the sun to filter through. The overhead glass was tinted a deep blue which gave a soft and wondrous light to everything below it. It filtered the harsh tropical sun and gave the aquarium an air of mystery. It was much like the reef underwater.

Ponce paused briefly to admire a miniature coral reef built along one side of the wall. It contained all the colorful sea fans and corals from the deep offshore waters. Ponce studied the indoor reef and its collection of undersea life including huge shells. Mr. Foster had even placed a pirate's chest on it, half open, with silver coins spilling out onto the sand. Two ancient cannons stuck up from the wooden timbers of an old wreck. It was a very pretty sight, Ponce admitted.

A girl his own age was at the counter today placing a roll of tickets into the cash register. She looked up as Ponce entered. No one else was there. She had long dark hair and an oval face. Her nose tilted up beneath long lashes and she wore a white sweater. A black minishirt and white boots made up the rest of her attire. Ponce liked the way Maria dressed.

"Hi, Maria," he said. "Are the fish doing well?"

She closed the register with a click, then pulled a lever down to clear it for the first customer. She smiled warmly at Ponce. Her day always brightened up when he stopped by the aquarium. He always brought new hope and confidence.

"We did not lose another one," she said. "Mr. Foster is in the laboratory dissecting the fishes that died." She flipped her head and long hair in the direction of the closed lab door. It was marked "PRIVATE." Ponce knew Mr. Foster was studying the fishes for tumors or other diseases of the fins. He was worried about pollution and had used his scientific skills to help combat it. Many fishes were showing up these days with odd growths on them which he said were caused by polluted waters.

"I will find him." Ponce walked through the small aisle made by a pipe railing and left Maria. Her eyes followed him. Ponce opened the lab door. He found the aged scientist busy over a metal operating table. In front of him lay several similar reef fish. He was working over them carefully with a scalpel. He glanced up as Ponce entered.

"I have come to fix the pipe," Ponce explained. He closed the door and surveyed the brightly lighted laboratory. There were scales for weighing fish, test tubes in racks, glass beakers, jars, and exhibit cases ranging along one wall. One of the larger jars held a dead octopus pickled in formaldehyde. Its glassy eyes glared from the brine. The tentacles and suction cups were magnified by the glass. Ponce noticed other jars held small fish, starfish, a squid, and some sea urchins with long needlelike black spines. The lab was an exciting place.

"I am looking for parasites," explained Mr. Foster. "I often find them in the stomachs." He ducked his white head and squinted along his spectacles through a powerful microscope. He soon forgot the young boy standing in the room.

"How is business today?" asked Ponce.

"Oh—all right, I guess," replied Mr. Foster, indicating he did not really know. He reached out for a test tube. Into it he poured some brown liquid. Ponce observed Mr. Foster's deep wrinkles on his pink face. They were creased like a prune except for his mouth, which had laugh lines etched into the corners. He never tanned, being indoors so much. Ponce rarely saw him outside on the Key West streets.

"Maybe more will come later," replied Ponce. "They would come even quicker if you had an act of some kind. You need something to lure them. A live act of some kind!"

"Maybe like turtle wrestling?" Mr. Foster raised his white head higher and studied Ponce cautiously. "You could wrestle turtles here!" He pushed his eyeglasses up on his forehead.

"No!" Ponce's voice rang firmly in the quiet of the lab. The air conditioner whined in the wall. "You don't have the room for it. None of your pens are large enough for me and a turtle. Also, it would not be fair. I do my wrestling at the Turtle Pens." He hoped that would end it.

Mr. Foster persisted. "I have large jewfish and black groupers out back off the docks. They are all in strong pens." He removed his eyeglasses and poked them into a pocket of his shirt. They were steamed up.

"I know that. I have even thought about it. But I don't like to swim with fish. And—what's more—I have an agreement with Mr. Waggle."

Mr. Foster turned back to his microscope. He knew Ponce would not ever wrestle at the aquarium. He could only hope the boy would come to work for him while he spent more time in the laboratory. It was important that he do his research. The world was dying slowly. Many seas were already dead. He forgot the boy again.

"I will fix the busted pipe," said Ponce.

"Thank you," replied Mr. Foster. "I appreciate very much what you did yesterday." He again stopped his work to stare at the young turtle wrestler. Ponce thought he looked like the ancient mariner. His blue eyes shone. His white hair was in disarray.

"It was nothing," confided the boy. "I do not like to see any fish die needlessly. Nor do I like for you to have trouble."

"It was a careless mistake."

"I am not convinced."

"Hmmmm."

"It was no accident, anyway." Ponce had resolved this in his mind, remembering the hammered shut valve. "It could happen again."

94

"I have no enemies," replied Mr. Foster.

"What about the advertising pamphlet you were going to publish?" Ponce asked, changing the subject. "Have you done it?" His voice took on a desperate tone. Mr. Foster shook his head from side to side.

Ponce continued: "Why do you spend so much time in the lab and not with the customers? They like to ask questions. You know so much about fish. It would be sort of a live act if you guided them."

"It is my way," wearily replied the old man. "I like the lab best."

Ponce's voice became harsh for the first time. "If your aquarium goes broke, so does the laboratory. Everything goes!"

Mr. Foster nodded assent. Ponce couldn't help comparing this quiet old man with blustery Cliff Waggle. They were completely different. One was businesslike and hard. The other soft and kind. And no good at business. He felt compassion for the white-haired scientist who labored so hard to help mankind.

"I'll go and fix the pipe," he mumbled. This time he left.

Mr. Foster hummed an old tune. His manner became more alert, and a small smile crossed his face as he worked. He had forgotten the words to the old tune. It was very old, like he was. He had to hum it in a jerky, singsong manner. He felt the boy and he had grown a little closer. He had Ponce concerned.

Ponce walked out onto the docks and entered the metal toolshed that leaned in a corner. On a rack he found a large wrench and a piece of unused pipe and put it in a bench vise. Then he picked up an electric drill and drilled a hole through the pipe. Into the hole he fitted a new lock valve. This would open or shut the air into the tanks. He killed the noisy compressor feeding air and went inside. He carried the pipe along with some metal sleeve couplers. Climbing up into the overhead pipes by a stepladder, he removed the soft rubber hose and put the new pipe section into the break. He sealed the coupled ends with a paste-like waterproof compound. The pipe fitted perfectly. It was strong.

Then he climbed down and put the stepladder away. He walked out back to the docks and started the air compressor. Bubbles began to flow into the tanks. He inspected each one before he left. All were bubbling merrily. The fishes stared out at him with goggle-eyes.

"Hey fish," he said. Then he looked around to make sure no one had heard him.

On his way outside he stopped to talk briefly with Maria. She had sweat droplets on her neck where her long hair hung. Everyone thought Maria a pretty girl, including Ponce. She was smart and a good worker. It was too bad she had to remain at the cash register. That left the dark aquarium empty and dark. It invited trouble, Ponce knew.

"Good bye," said Ponce.

"So long," replied Maria with a flash of her dark eyes. "Come again."

"Try to keep an eye inside," Ponce warned her. "I am afraid Mr. Foster has an enemy."

She looked at him. "I try," she said. "It's not easy."

"I know," replied the boy wrestler. "I fixed the pipe. Again."

"I know, Ponce," Maria said. "I wish you worked here."

"I would miss the action," the boy replied.

"There may be more action here if Mr. Foster has an enemy."

"I hope not. I'm running out of energy."

Maria laughed loudly. Ponce had his joking moments. He was mostly too serious, she thought. She liked him when he was lighthearted. She saw him smile and slip out the front door.

Ponce stopped briefly at the Tourist Train to talk to Jorge. He found him busy wiping the shiny metal on the engine. Jorge was delighted to see Ponce. He stopped wiping and asked:

"The turtle—how is it?"

"Very much alive. And very strong."

"I told my family how we caught it," Jorge bragged. "They said we were . . . were . . ."

"Nuts?" asked Ponce.

"Well, something like that. It was a family shock." Jorge smiled and wiped his hot face with the greasy rag, leaving a smudge on his cheek.

"I know," Ponce answered. "You were very brave in the boat."

Jorge flushed at the compliment. He bent to his polishing as though the bright train might rust before his eyes. A banyan tree threw shade on the cars now filling with tourists. It was a pleasant place to work and a secure summer job. Ponce frowned.

"I have to go now to hand out literature," Jorge said, sliding down the engine.

"How many tourists?" Ponce asked.

"Plenty. Already most of the seats are sold. We pick up more at the hotel on the way. We are always full."

Ponce glanced at the train and noticed what Jorge said was true. It was filling rapidly for its city-wide tour. It became clear to the boy turtle wrestler that the Tourist Train paid off well. Business at the Turtle Pens seemed to be growing too. Only the aquarium seemed to suffer by comparison.

Ponce left and proceeded home to have lunch with his father. As he walked along the streets his mind raced with many confusing thoughts. He didn't realize it, but he had forgotten his own problems. The aquarium had taken up most of his mind.

The Tourist Train passed him halfway home. It tooted its horn as it went by. Jorge hung on the rear end grinning. He waved to Ponce. Ponce waved back. It was a half-hearted wave. The train disappeared down the street as people scampered out of its way.

17

Ponce arrived home before his father came home from his work at the Chamber of Commerce and began to fix their lunch. He cut two halves of an avocado and cooked some yellow Spanish rice in hot water. Into the rice he cut some green and red peppers. These grew on a bush in his back yard. The peppers gave the rice flavor and spice. He also picked some yellow key limes off a tree.

Señor Alvarez came into the house about twelve thirty and greeted his son more cheerfully than he had in many a day. He laughed and joked and Ponce wondered if his father had received a promotion.

Señor Alvarez walked across the room and hung his hat on the wall mirror rimmed with dark wood that had pegs sticking out from the edges. He took off his shiny black silk coat and loosened his black cord tie before sitting down at the table spread with food.

As was his custom, Ponce waited for his father to speak. He noticed his father had whistled between his teeth most of the time he walked around the room. This meant he had some idea, or secret, on his mind. Ponce ate, watching his father between bites.

"Where is the olive oil?" his father finally asked.

Ponce leaped up and brought the oil in the colorful red and green can. He set it on the table and then sat down again. The waiting was unbearable. It was good news because of the whistling. When it was bad, his father remained silent.

Señor Alvarez coughed and wiped his mouth. The food was very tasty, and he smiled at Ponce in appreciation. He took a drink of the limeade the boy had fixed and put some fresh lime on his avocado. Then he salted and peppered it. It seemed to him they grew most of their own food in the backyard.

"Have you heard our good news?" he finally asked.

"No," said Ponce. "I was at the Turtle Pens and the aquarium. I heard nothing new."

Señor Alvarez wiped his mouth again. "The Chamber of Commerce is going to help license a new boat to carry tourists to Yucatán. It will carry many people and cars to Mexico." He paused and leaned back. "I am in charge of the arrangements to help the new owners."

Ponce's eyes opened wider. "That's good," he said. "The boat must be large."

"Very large. One-hundred-ten feet. It carries cars on the back end like a ferry boat. It will help Key West very much since the U.S. Navy is cutting down its base. It will bring more tourists and help employment."

They both ate their rice and avocado in silence. For a moment, they were very close to each other. Talk between them was usually a few words. They sensed each other's emotions. It was such a time now.

"And how did it go for you today?" asked Ponce's

100

father. His dark brows curled upward at the question.

"Not well," replied the boy. "The turtle is bigger and wiser than I had realized. He will be difficult to tame."

Ponce had always spoken truthfully to his father even though it was sometimes hard to do so. He did not bend the truth to his needs. His father knew that.

"Too bad." Señor Alvarez leaned back. "He is a very old one and set in his ways. I have heard he is truly huge!" He raised an eyebrow.

Ponce changed the subject. He knew what his father was leading up to. "I also fixed the pipe at the aquarium. It is like new now."

This made him think again of Mr. Foster in his laboratory. He wondered if he would remember to eat his midday meal. Maybe he should take him an avocado after lunch. It would not be out of his way. Often Mr. Foster forgot to eat when he was busy.

Señor Alvarez rose from his chair. "Would you like to see the plans for the new boat?" He asked. He walked over to his coat and reached inside. From an inner pocket he took out a rolled paper drawing.

Ponce pushed the dishes aside on the table so there would be room. Señor Alvarez crossed the room leisurely and sat down at the table. He took the rolled-up drawing and spread it out before them.

Ponce walked around the table and leaned down beside his father. Before him lay the brightly colored picture of a boat. It was done in water colors and looked very much like a magazine photograph. The boat had two decks and he noticed its broad beam. There were many windows down the sides as the decks were glass enclosed against weather. The rear end was open for cars to roll on from the pier.

"It will carry more than one hundred tourists at a time," stated his father.

"Whew," said Ponce.

"I met a man on the street and he asked me where the Chamber of Commerce was. I told him I worked there and could I help him. He showed me the boat and told me about his plans. Now I am in charge of helping to get him publicity in the papers and a place to dock it."

"Your name will be in the paper," replied his son.

"Yes, I assume so," said Señor Alvarez, straightening up. "I shall go to Mexico on the first trip too."

Ponce's eyes brightened. He liked to see his father doing so well in his work. It made him forget the turtle and his own problems. He watched as his father rolled the paper up and replaced it inside his coat. Then he cleaned off the table and washed the dishes. Afterward he wrapped an avocado in a piece of foil.

"What is that for?" asked his father.

"I thought I'd drop it off at the aquarium," said Ponce.

"Ah, yes," said Señor Alvarez. He smiled. He knew why his son was doing it, but did not question him further. Soon the screen door banged and Ponce had left. It was a good day. He thought Key West was a very nice town in which to live and work. Ponce was a part of the joy.

Ponce headed down the streets toward the aquarium once again.

18

Ponce found Mr. Foster busy in the aquarium working on a new exhibit tank containing live crawfish. The marine tank before Ponce's eyes gleamed with light and beauty. The spiny crawfish were hiding in holes of a small coral reef which had been constructed inside the tank. A jagged branch of white staghorn coral jutted up in the center. From the coral several red and orange and white and purple-toned sea anemones waved their colorful arms. They looked like flowers to the young turtle wrestler.

Ponce handed Mr. Foster the avocado. He thanked the boy and stuck it into his coat pocket. Then he explained what he was trying to do in the exhibit tank.

"I have been trying to clear the water with a new type of bottom filter. First I run the water through sand and through a gauze trap set into a ring. The sand and gauze clear the impurities out. Does it not look clearer?" He stepped back to study the brightly-lighted tank.

The tank, Ponce noted, did look clearer than the others. It was almost like looking through air. "Yes," Ponce replied. "I think you have it licked."

Mr. Foster rubbed his nose with pleasure. He was always puttering inside the aquarium trying to improve the looks of the tanks and fish displays. Since the recent trouble with the air pipe Ponce felt a protective attitude toward the old scientist. He had never felt it so strongly before. Something inside him had changed lately.

When Mr. Foster had satisfied himself with the appearance of the tank, he walked outside with Ponce to the docks at the rear of the building. These docks hung out over the water and were wired beneath to keep live fish in outdoor pens. The square-holed wire was attached to the pilings that held the docks up. At the rail of one of these outside pens Ponce and Mr. Foster stood while Mr. Foster ate his avocado. As he ate Ponce stared down at the large jewfish swimming below in the deep water. Something about them bothered him.

The trouble with the outdoor tank was that the fish were so huge their movements kept the water partly clouded, as their tails stirred up the bottom mud. At times Ponce caught a good view of a brown-speckled back. The flash looked like sunlight glancing off metal. Then the muddy water became normal.

Mr. Foster was talking but Ponce barely heard him. Before his startled eyes he saw a large jewfish swim out of the pen and into the open harbor. With a quick flick of its massive tail it was gone.

Ponce seized Mr. Foster by his arm. He said in alarm. "A jewfish just swam out. The wire must be broken!"

Mr. Foster put his white head far over the railing and looked down, staring at the spot where Ponce pointed. The water cleared and they at once saw the situation. Another jewfish approached the wire and seemed to melt through it. Then he too was gone. Each fish weighed about five hundred pounds. Neither Ponce nor the aquarium owner could see the actual break in the mesh due to the depth and cloudiness of the water. But it had to be a break. Both of them had seen the fish escape into deeper water. Soon none of the valuable specimens would be left in the pen if the hole were not plugged.

Mr. Foster looked around in wild abandon. "What will we ever do?" he asked in a helpless tone. He glanced around the docks to see what he could discover that might be used to block up the hole. Nothing large enough was around. He moved down the railing looking for anything, even a heavy net.

Ponce let him wander. As Mr. Foster moved away the boy wrestler slipped a leg over the railing and poised for a moment on the edge of the dock above the water. Then he dove into the deep harbor outside the wire pens. In a second he was gone. Mr. Foster turned in surprise at the splash and ran up to the spot. Ponce had already disappeared into the murky water.

It took Ponce a few seconds to get his eyes accustomed to the silted water. Then he began to see things fuzzily. First he saw the gray mud bottom below him. Then he was swimming among the pilings of the dock which looked like bare trees under the water. They were covered with moss and had barnacles growing on them.

He turned and swam among the forest of pilings and approached the wire net. The mesh appeared intact, covered with a green algae. The soft mossy growth hid the hard steel of the net. He felt along it, pulling his body through the water. As he crawled along the wire he kept looking ahead for the break.

Then Ponce saw the divers. There were two of them. Both had on aqualungs and face masks. They had a pair of large wire cutters with which they were busy cutting the netlike wire mesh. Evidently they intended to have all the fish escape from the outdoor exhibit pen. Mr. Foster would lose all the valuable jewfish.

The water where Ponce had dived was fifteen feet deep. This depth and his search along the wire for the hole had made him feel dizzy due to lack of air. Still unnoticed, he floated to the surface where he bobbed into view before Mr. Foster's worried gaze. He emerged in a cloud of bubbles and foam.

"Divers," he gasped. "They are cutting the wire to let all the fish out." He breathed hard. The air felt good in his lungs. It revived him quickly. His years on the reef had equipped him well for this sort of emergency.

Taking in a long deep breath, Ponce dived and headed immediately for the break in the net. He wasted no time. As he arrived he found only one diver busy working. The other had swum away out of sight. Now the diver saw Ponce for the first time. He tried to kick his way free from the wire mesh and in doing so dropped his wire cutters in alarm. He had not expected this.

Ponce reasoned that the first diver had spotted him and attempted to give his partner a warning before swimming away. But the diver Ponce now encountered had not understood. Thus he had been caught in the act. He turned quickly to face the strong, brown boy swimming toward him with powerful strokes. Ponce saw his face through the glass mask. He was young, a boy his own age.

Ponce caught the diver with his back to the wire. The two met head on and their arms locked in combat. They wrestled, locked together like two giant crabs fighting over a piece of fish. Although the diver had the advantage of the face mask and aqualung, he was no match for the boy who hade a living wrestling sea turtles.

106

The two sank toward the bottom heavy with silt. Soon Ponce could not see because of the silt their feet kicked up. He wished now he had the advantage of at least a face mask. His lungs hurt and a feeling of panic struck him. Suppose he had taken on too much? The diver could breathe beneath water.

Ponce felt the weight of the diver on top of him. He was pushing Ponce down into the soft bottom. Ponce saw red flashes in front of his eyes. He felt himself growing weaker. Only his natural movements under water were saving him. He knew the diver could not see either now with the silt in the water around them. He knew he must act. Quickly.

He reached toward the diver's head much like he did the big loggerhead. Then he felt for the mask. His hands moved along the diver's shoulders to his neck. They felt the chin and the rubber hose gripped in the mouth. It was flexible in Ponce's grasp. With a wrench he tore it loose. It made a loud bubbling noise as it came out. The diver gulped water. Ponce felt him stiffen in fear. He relaxed his hold on Ponce. His thoughts were only for air. He fought for the surface in desperation. Ponce could not hold him.

Ponce let him go and rose behind him to the surface.

On the top Ponce sucked in air hungrily. His arms and body ached with the long submersion and fight. But he swam over to the frightened diver spitting out muddy water and seized his shoulders. He flipped him onto his back and towed him over to the docks. Ponce felt soft hands grip on his arms. Then he was yanked out of the water and shortly sat dripping on the dry boards. He too gulped air.

A considerable crowd had gathered. Ponce saw several police uniforms in the crowd. They took the diver by his arms and lifted him off the boards where he lay collapsed. Silt and muddy water still ran out of his mouth. His color was gray and his eyes remained closed. His chest rose and fell with labored breathing. The police carried him inside.

Mr. Foster helped Ponce to his feet. "I ran for the police when you first came up," he explained. "A patrol car was outside by the Tourist Train. They came quickly." Ponce nodded weakly and attempted a bright smile. He was overly tired. He still could not get his breath under control long enough to speak. He nodded his head. He realized Mr. Foster had acted wisely in calling the police so as to apprehend the diver. The second diver had evidently escaped. No doubt he would climb ashore down by the Navy Base and disappear into the island city. He would look like any other Navy frogman.

He stood up. He and Mr. Foster walked inside the aquarium and approached the laboratory. It was here the police had taken the diver. Ponce noticed now the diver was wearing a tightly fitting wet suit. It was all black. He had on rubber swim fins. The air tanks had been removed from his back by the police who sat him in a chair where he slumped forward, his arms on his knees.

In build he was was somewhat thicker than Ponce, but not nearly as muscled. This had made the difference underwater in the fight. Anger flashed in Ponce's face as he stared at the diver who had pushed him into the mud intent on drowning him. He glared hard. But the diver lowered his head. He hung his head in shame studying the floor.

Ponce heard the police asking questions. The diver said his name was Alfred Bates and that he was seventeen. Ponce hadn't realized he was that old! He looked at Mr. Foster and raised his eyebrows. Mr. Foster smiled back in acknowledgment. Ponce now knew how hard the fight underwater had been.

108

The frightened diver talked freely now that he had been caught. Ponce had nearly drowned him. His words were shaky, but he spoke the truth. His underwater friend had deserted him. Sitting there in his wet trunks with water streaming onto the floor, the diver felt insecure. His bravado had vanished.

The police had drawn from him that he and his accomplice had been hired by an old fisherman on Little Torch Key. He had told them to cut the aquarium wire mesh. A policeman, named Frank, spoke:

"You know this man?" His tone was accusing.

"Francisco. Francisco Valdez," the diver said. He raised his black eyes.

Mr. Foster became alert at the mention of the name. His blue eyes grew bright as he heard it. The enemy was out in the open. Now he knew who was out to ruin him.

"I know this man," he said as police officer Frank turned to him, pencil poised above his notebook. "He used to work for me. Let's see. That must have been several years ago." He stroked his chin in reflection.

"Does this man have anything against you?"

Mr. Foster thought more deeply. His eyes studied the floor as though the answer might be found in the tiles. He recalled that the man had sold him live fish specimens. Then he raised his white head and spoke.

"I do recall one thing," he said. "The man smuggled perfume in from Cuba and used my dock as a landing place. He always thought I turned him in when he was arrested. He got a year in jail."

Now Ponce knew why the air valve had been tampered with. Also he knew why the pasty-faced, red haired kid had worked there. Also why the divers had come to Key West. It was clear now that Mr. Foster did have an enemy he had forgotten about. It was very good he had dived into the water to see why the fish were escaping. In this way he had caught the divers at work and brought the whole situation to a head.

Ponce felt important. It was a sense of having accomplished something of true value, unlike the thrills of wrestling the sea turtles in the pens. This feeling brought an inner satisfaction that he had never known.

The police soon learned from the captured diver that Francisco Valdez docked at Little Torch Key. There was a close-in channel and a tiny beach on the Gulf side. The rest was mangrove jungle. It was a lonely fish camp, he said.

The policeman approached Ponce and Mr. Foster. He had put away his notebook and hitched his pants higher over his stomach. His gun swung from a holster on his hip. It was silver plated and had pearl handle grips. "We'll go to Little Torch and see if we can find this man," said Frank. "Can you both go with us?"

They went outside to the two shiny police cars now pulled up in front of the aquarium. Ponce and Mr. Foster climbed into the rear seat of one car. The diver was put into the other. The cars had blue flashing lights atop their roofs.

Frank turned on the police band radio. Ponce heard him advise headquarters that they were stopping by for the prisoner to be booked. Then they sped off, the blue lights flashing as they went down the narrow Key West streets. The lights were like warning beacons at sea, thought Ponce.

The stop at the police station was tiresome. Ponce fretted at the delay. Frank had gone inside and stayed for awhile. Ponce was worried that the second diver would have had time to warn Francisco Valdez. The police were taking too long, he thought. Little Torch Key was thirty minutes away.

Finally Frank emerged and sauntered to the car door. He took off his cap and wiped his hot forehead with a white handkerchief. He stepped inside, remarking how hot it was today. "Sorry about the delay," he said. "There was much paper work to do first."

"I hope we can still catch him," replied Mr. Foster, also worried at the delay.

"All our patrols were in Key West. There were none we could radio between here and Marathon," said officer Frank.

Ponce shrugged. They had caught one diver and uncovered a plot. That much had been done to break up the ring.

Soon they sped north along the highway. The car worked its way out of the cramped Key West traffic and flashed beside the charter boat fishing docks beneath tall coconut palms. Hot dog and root beer signs flashed past. Then a number of gasoline stations. Soon they were on U.S. 1, their light blinking a warning as they sped across concrete bridges and over the busy highway that led from the island city.

It took a half hour to reach deserted Little Torch Key. Ponce calculated that they had taken two hours since he had first caught the divers at work in the water. The police car turned into a white marl road cut through the mangroves. It curved slightly to the right and then suddenly burst out onto a clearing holding a wood shack and a rickety fishing dock piled high with nets. A flapping canvas banged and clattered in a vacant window. A gray heron squawked and rose up into the air with noisy wings. A raccoon slid off into mangrove roots.

111

Then Ponce saw the boat. It was an old double-end lifeboat with a canvas canopy raised on four poles overhead for shade. It was already far from the dock and leaving fast. The tiny figure under the canvas was evidently Francisco Valdez. He had escaped.

The policeman gave the boat a brief glance and then poked around the camp looking for evidence. The campsite was cut out of the stilt-rooted mangroves and there was a small open beach in front. The water crept up close to the hut and into the mangroves on each side. Offshore there were similar green islands in the blue bay. Many of them. The boat soon hid among the nearest islands and was gone.

"I am sorry that I do not have a boat," said Frank. "Possibly the Coast Guard can pick him up later. We will need some evidence, though."

"Do now worry," said Mr. Foster. "I am sure we will not have anything to fear anymore. This has been a lesson to him."

"I agree with that," said Officer Frank.

"Ponce chased them all off," said Mr. Foster.

The police officer smiled. Ponce smiled back. It was true. What he had done was good enough.

"The country of the Ten Tousand Islands is a perfect place to hide," Ponce remarked. "Valdez will get lost in them and make his way up the west coast to Cedar Key or Sanibel. We shall not hear from him again."

As they rewound their way to the highway along the marl road the radio crackled out many messages about traffic violations. The officer listened to them laconically. Then he picked up the mouthpiece and, as they swung onto the highway, talked into it, telling the female operator they were returning to Key West without a prisoner.

"Over and out," he said.

"Roger," replied the girl with the nice voice on the radio. "Loud and clear. Ten-forty."

They passed Big Coppit Key and the U.S. Naval Air Station with its fat, hot metal hangars. Drab colored jet planes stood in the sun with their wings folded back like sea gulls. Soon the car crossed a bridge and they came to Key West and its tiny homes.

On the way to the aquarium where they would drop Mr. Foster they passed the Turtle Pens. Ponce gave a sidelong glance. Inside the giant loggerhead waited.

19

Business had picked up at the Turtle Pens. Tourists flocked to see the boy turtle wrestler fight his big turtle. Word had spread around. Waggle and the turtle workers hung over the railing, watching. Sally fretted alone in the gift shop. It was just like the old days. Only more exciting.

Each day Ponce climbed down into the pen and spent several hours mornings and afternoons in the water with the sea beast. They knew each other well now. Every day was the same. Ponce lost the battle. The turtle was too smart or too large for him.

Each day Ponce climbed out more discouraged than before. The turtle had now become an obsession with him. He fought it by day in the pens and at night in his sleep. Daily the loggerhead became weaker. It had refused all food, even Charley's squid. It was in rebellion. It hated the cage and often butted its shell against the outer boards. It fought everything in sight.

Ponce did not want to starve the sea turtle into submission. The fight, he told himself, was not worthwhile unless he tamed the loggerhead on equal terms. The thought that his turtle might even die crossed his mind. He shook his head. That would be a tragedy.

He had even grown fond of the turtle. It was different than their fight at sea. There they had met as strangers. In the pens they tested each other daily while hundreds of people watched. A bond had grown between the boy and his loggerhead. Ponce was sure, though, that the bond was one-sided.

Several days his friends showed up at the pens. But each left sadly and with a word of encouragement. Each was busy now at his own job. They could not stay. Ponce was glad to see them. He climbed out and joked with them. He sat on the railing and watched the sea turtle as they talked. Then he plunged into the cool green water again to try to conquer the ancient sea turtle.

Jorge rode the Tourist Train all day long, handing out literature and shining the brass parts. He came to see Ponce during lunch. Miguel and Marco had resumed normal lives. Afternoons Marco played baseball and Miguel spent most of his time painting his family's house, or milking his goat. One day Miguel dropped by to greet his friend, Ponce, and offer some hope.

"He is very cunning," he confided to Ponce after watching the wild battle in the water below.

"This one has me worried," replied Ponce, climbing out onto the dock from the wooden ladder. He sat down, dripping water. It spread out around him on the hot dry boards like an ink spot. "He attacks me with his beak. I could easily lose a hand. He is so quick."

"Aiye!"

"Or an arm!"

"That would be very bad."

"I wonder what he thinks." Ponce studied the turtle.

"He thinks that freedom is worth an arm. Even yours."

"Maybe," said Ponce. "He is fighting harder. Freedom means life to him. Life at sea."

"Doing what he wants," said Miguel.

"Yes."

"Like you."

"Yes."

Ponce stared hard at Miguel. He noticed his half-smile. It was true. He and the turtle were very much alike. Both were in a rebellious mood and wanted freedom more than anything. They each loved the sea. They each were caged. They fought. Strong forces held them both.

"I must go," said Miguel.

"Thanks a lot," replied Ponce. He watched Miguel walk off. But it was true. He stood up and shook himself. Only one could emerge the victor, he told himself. He wondered if it would be him. Looking at the turtle below in the pen he wondered again if it could be subdued. Ever.

That evening he talked it over with his father at home. His father drank some black Cuban coffee. Ponce sipped ice tea.

"I may lose the battle," he said to his father.

"And win," the old man said.

"I guess," replied Ponce. "I do not wish to hurt the turtle. It is I who captured and penned him. He must hate me. But I do not hate him."

"There are many pens in life," said Señor Alvarez. "Many of our own making even."

Ponce thought awhile and then went to bed. The next day he would wrestle again.

Then it happened. That afternoon Ponce had been in the water for an hour battling the turtle before a large crowd when the turtle turned quickly. Ponce had seized its shell and was spread across its back. Then it threw him off in the water, helpless. It turned again and came at him. Ponce saw its eyes bulging with rage.

He had no time to call out. As he thrashed about in confusion, the turtle hit him wide open. Its beak opened and it went for his arm much like it had the barracuda it had bitten in half. But Ponce moved too quickly. He swung away at just the right moment and the sharp beak cut only skin. The turtle then swam into him, hitting his thigh. The strange hornlike hook on its front flipper caught in Ponce's trunks. It held. The loggerhead submerged, and Ponce felt himself being dragged down and down into the coolness of the depths.

He held onto the turtle's back. He hit it with one arm and tried to kick with his feet as the loggerhead raced ahead. It crashed with great force into the rotten outer posts and they buckled. Then it hit the posts again and dragged Ponce through the jagged opening. His lungs aching, he felt the turtle pull free. He swam weakly to the surface, bleeding from an arm wound and bruised about the body. Ponce gasped for air, treading water.

Dimly he heard the crowd above him shout: "The boy. He has been bitten by the turtle. Get a doctor."

Charley King and several other men from the cannery appeared, pushing their way through the crowd. Leaning over the outside of the pen they seized Ponce's body. The world seemed to explode in his brain and then he knew nothing. Eager hands hauled him up onto the safety of the dock.

When Ponce regained consciousness he was in Waggle's office. He lay on a couch. He saw his right arm was bandaged. He also saw Sally nervously biting her nails. Waggle was there too. He saw him dimly.

"How yew feel, boy?" Waggle asked, a new warmth in his voice.

Ponce sat up. His arm throbbed with pain but his head was not clear. Then he remembered the turtle. "The turtle? Where?" The last he recalled was the rotting timbers crashing around him.

"It got clean away," said Waggle.

"Good riddance," said Sally. Waggle cautioned her to be quiet. He knew the strong feeling Ponce had for the sea turtle.

"It's okay," said Ponce. "I became careless. At least he won what he wanted. His freedom."

"I should think—"

"Shut up, Sally." Waggle meant it this time.

"You fit him well, Ponce." It was Charley. He looked up and saw Charley King who brought the turtle fish and squid every day. He was smiling down at the injured Ponce. "I'll hep you to yore feet."

He offered Ponce a hand and the boy stood erect. The dizziness left him and he felt strong again. Only the hurt arm throbbed. The shorts were badly torn on one side by the hook on the flipper. But they still held together. Ponce noticed he had lost his knife. He had never once thought to use it.

"The old boards finally gave way," reported Waggle. "The old turtle had been working on them all night. I heard him once when I came back to work late." He banged them all night long."

"I am glad something gave," laughed Ponce. "I did not like going out that way, for sure." He smiled at the small group in the cool office. Everyone laughed. Then he straightened and began to walk to the door. Waggle seized an arm and helped him. They went together through the

118

patio and the gift shop. Some tourists were watching. On
the street Waggle asked Ponce if he could make it alone.
The boy nodded. He paused a moment.

"I was mixed up about the turtle," Ponce explained.

"Take your time, son," said the Turtle Pen owner. "It's a
long road ahead."

"What shall I do?"

"I don't know, Ponce. You're now a man. It is your
own decision to make." He spoke quickly and firmly,
offering the young boy no easy way. He knew Ponce had
to make the decision for himself. It was more than losing
the turtle. He had to decide for himself.

Ponce faced Waggle. Then he blurted out: "I do not
want to wrestle sea turtles any more!"

That was what Waggle feared to hear. He knew it was
coming and he did not want to lose Ponce. But he could
not force him to stay. Like Captain Anderson said—"How
long you going to hold the boy in bondage?" He had been
thinking mostly of himself and his business. He had been
using the boy, unfairly.

"The turtle has won," Waggle said. "Over both of us."

"No," said Ponce. "It was wrong capturing such an old
one. He had lived too long free. I could never have tamed
him." He stared down at his bare feet.

"I see." Waggle clamped down on his cigar. He was a
powerful man used to having his way. But the boy was
winning now. And he wanted him to. It was a strange
feeling he felt.

"I won't hold you anymore," Waggle said. He took the
cigar out of his mouth and faced Ponce. "I guess you'll go
to work at the aquarium now?" He looked closely into
Ponce's face.

"Yes," Ponce replied softly. "Mr. Foster can use me.

And it will please my father." He looked down the street.

Waggle smiled. They were both in better spirits.

"Go," said Waggle, clapping Ponce hard on the back. He got a little redder in the face and turned his head. Then he stuck out his heavy hand. They both shook and Ponce turned and sailed off down the street.

Ponce felt no pain from his injuries as he ran down the street in his bare feet. He almost crashed head-on into two old ladies who were walking on the sidewalk window shopping. "Sorry," he called out. Then he was gone.

"Lands sake," said one of the ladies, rearranging her straw hat. "I wonder if that young boy knows where he is going?"

"I doubt it," said the other. "Today's children are . . ."

Ponce was out of earshot. He didn't stop running until he raced through the open ray mouth of the Oceanic Aquarium.

Maria looked up as he rushed in. "Gosh," she said. "What brings you here in such a rush?"

"A loggerhead," said Ponce. "Just a turtle." He grinned his widest.

Then he disappeared inside.